MURDER AT BRIGHTON BEACH

A GINGER GOLD MYSTERY #13

LEE STRAUSS

Library and Archives Canada Cataloguing in Publication

Title: Murder at Brighton Beach / Lee Strauss.

Names: Strauss, Lee (Novelist), author.

Series: Strauss, Lee (Novelist). Ginger Gold mystery ; 13.

Description: Series statement: A Ginger Gold mystery ; 13 | "A 1920s cozy historical mystery."

Identifiers: Canadiana (print) 20200228501 | Canadiana (ebook) 2020022851X | ISBN 9781774091067

(hardcover) | ISBN 9781774091081 (softcover) | ISBN 9781774091074 (IngramSpark softcover) | ISBN

9781774091098 (Kindle) | ISBN 9781774091104 (EPUB)

Classification: LCC PS8637.T739 M78 2020 | DDC C813/.6—dc23

GINGER GOLD MYSTERIES

(IN ORDER)

*M*rs. Ginger Reed gripped her husband's arm. Overcome with a nasty urge to vomit, she tried to steady herself to no avail. Her husband, Basil Reed, a chief inspector at Scotland Yard, stared down at her. His handsome face was etched with concern, his warm hazel eyes, round in question. "You're not—"

Ginger held a gloved hand to her mouth and mumbled. "Uh-huh." The former Lady Gold had been certain that she'd suffer mildly whilst travelling from London to Brighton in the afternoon—however, the mornings were the worst times. As she stared at the front entrance of the Victorian-style Brighton Seaside Hotel, she sensed the worst possible thing was about to happen.

Reaching for the first thing that would suit the

present crisis, Basil grabbed a pot of pansies from the windowsill and held it by Ginger's face. Ginger inhaled as she focused on the fragrance of the blossoms and not the bubbling acid in her stomach. She couldn't possibly be sick in a flowerpot belonging to the management of the Brighton Seaside Hotel!

As it was, she'd already soiled Basil's trilby on the train trip down—the stylish hat had had to be discarded at the last station.

Thankfully, the emergency passed, and she postponed further humiliation. But her eleven-year-old adopted son, Scout; her sister-in-law, Felicia Gold; and the Dowager Lady Gold, Ginger's grandmother-in-law, circled her with expressions of various degrees of mortification. Technically, Felicia and Ambrosia were no longer related to Ginger since the association had been with Ginger's late husband, Daniel, Lord Gold. But to Ginger, they would always be family, and the two Gold ladies resided with Ginger and Basil at Hartigan House, their home in South Kensington. Boss, Ginger's black-and-white Boston terrier, sat obediently on the pavement, staring up at his owner with round brown eyes.

Standing back from the group were two maids— Lizzie, petite with a pixie face, who worked for Ginger, and Langley, Ambrosia's tall and sombre-faced lady's maid.

"Are you all right, Ginger?" Felicia asked. A decade Ginger's junior, Felicia wore a flowered chiffon day dress with a flaring tunic trimmed in ribbon and a matching skirt with scalloped tiers. Her pretty face—made-up with thin arches for brows, two pinkish circles on her cheeks, and red bow-like lips—flushed with something akin to dread. Not because Ginger was ill unto death, though she sometimes felt like it, but because she'd behaved uncharacteristically emotionally. Since she'd learned a baby was on the way—a tremendously happy surprise—Ginger had to confess she hadn't quite been herself.

"Yes," Ginger said, throwing her shoulders back. "I'm fine. The danger has passed."

Ambrosia, standing more stiffly than a lady her age was meant to, had refused to consider leaving her corset behind and stubbornly insisted on dealing with the heat of this mid-June day by dabbing at her brow with a lace handkerchief. Leaning on a silver-handled walking stick, she sniffed. "Didn't I say that travelling at this juncture of your delicacy was a bad idea?"

"I'm fine, Grandmother," Ginger insisted. It'd been Basil's suggestion they get away from London for a little relaxation, and Ginger had agreed. "I'm already invigorated by the sea air." She turned to Basil and smiled. "Thank you for bringing us here."

Basil's eyes sparkled with fondness, and Ginger felt entirely cared for.

"Let's get checked in then, shall we?" he said.

A porter opened the main doors, and Basil tipped him to bring in the stack of suitcases, trunks, and hat boxes delivered to the kerb by the three taxicab drivers it had taken to transport the Reed-Gold clan to the hotel.

In jest, he'd muttered into Ginger's ear, "I thought we were staying for a week, not a month."

"A lady can never be too prepared," Ginger had returned. "A woman never knows what type of occasion she will be called to attend, and with the beach, there are extra outfits and costumes not normally needed elsewhere."

The decision to take a family holiday had been rather impromptu, and Ginger had had little time to plan. Owning Feathers & Flair, her Regent Street dress shop, had made matters infinitely easier. She had made a telephone call to her competent manager, the fabulous Madame Roux, who pulled together an appropriate wardrobe.

The interior design of the Brighton Seaside Hotel was deliriously delightful. It was a grand house belonging to the well-heeled Winthrop family, who, since the war, had made America their home. Ginger thought the transformation into a luxurious, though small hotel, was a financially expedient move—certainly to earn more money for the family than simply renting it out—since the Brighton area was a coveted place for the English to holiday.

Carpeted with a luxurious tapestry design over polished hardwood floors, the entrance was vast. An impressive staircase wound up four storeys with an ornate greenish-blue railing of oxidised copper. Multiple chandeliers hung from high ceilings, which were lavishly decorated with carved mouldings.

The maids forgot themselves momentarily, letting expressions of disbelief wash over their plain faces. Scout, who'd only just recently adjusted to a life of means and who thought Hartigan House was a palace, grabbed Ginger's hand. "I've never seen such a sight, Mum."

Felicia let out a giggle of delight and turned to Basil. "How frightfully right you were, Basil. This was such a grand idea!"

Ambrosia shot Ginger a look, her pinched lips and wrinkled-faced nod a clear sign that the Dowager Lady Gold was eager to sign in and get to her room. Ginger nudged Basil who approached the reception desk.

"Reservation for Reed."

A middle-aged man with thin dark hair oiled back over a round head, looked up. His pencil-thin moustache stretched out over a broad smile which wrinkled in the shape of a parenthesis at the corner of his lips. Dressed in the crisp black uniform of the manager, he held both hands clasped behind his back. With a slight bow, he replied, "Absolutely, sir. I'm Mr. Floyd, the manager here at the Brighton Seaside Hotel, and I'm at your service." He ran a finger down the page of the opened registry book. "Yes, here it is. Party of five, and two lady's maids."

With a dollop of physical effort, the porter who'd greeted them at the door pushed the luggage trolley, overfilled with the Reed party's belongings, towards the lift. With swift, short strides, Mr. Floyd approached the lad. "Second floor, suites two and three."

The porter lifted his chin in acknowledgement and proceeded on his journey.

Once Basil had signed in the appropriate places, he asked the manager, "Where might I find a hatter? I've lost one of mine," he explained graciously, "and I'd like to purchase another. A keepsake to remind me of our visit here."

"There is a shop next door to the hotel, sir, that sells hats for men," Mr. Floyd said. "You'll find it and other convenient establishments along the promenade." Handing Basil the room keys, he added, "If you'd like to wait a few minutes, the lift should be free. Please direct the porter to place your luggage exactly where you'd like it. I know you've brought your own maids—their room is on the attic floor—but should you need to call them, the suites have an efficient bell system. Mrs. Gwen Merrick, the housekeeper, will assign chambermaids for daily room attendance."

"Thank you," Basil said.

The maids were directed to the staff staircase, leaving the five to head towards the lift. The attendant opened brass gates on the lift doors and said to a lady getting out, "Have a good afternoon, Mrs. Bainbridge."

Bainbridge. The name rang a tone of familiarity in Ginger's mind. Hadn't she read that name in the newspapers? Ginger tried to remember the article. *That was it! A man by that name had gone missing recently in this region—had he been staying at this very hotel?*

The young lady held a glove to her face, her eyes gazing downward. Eagerly, she darted out of the lift, into the lobby and straight into Ginger.

"Oh, please excuse me," Mrs. Bainbridge said.

Ginger noted the lady's teary eyes and unflattering frown. A silk oriental-print shawl with its long fringe was wrapped around her shoulders and didn't conceal that the straight-line tunic of her frock pulled snugly against a rounded stomach. *Mrs. Bainbridge is with child.* Ginger felt an immediate affinity.

"It's quite all right," Ginger said. To Basil, she

added quickly, "This lift isn't large enough for all of us. I'll wait for it to return."

Basil's hazel-eyed gaze moved from Ginger to Mrs. Bainbridge and back, then flashed with understanding.

Ginger loved how her husband knew her so well! He perceived that she wanted to talk to Mrs. Bainbridge.

"I'll wait too," Felicia said. The lift only held four people comfortably, and the attendant took up one of those spaces.

"Mrs. Bainbridge," Ginger called out.

At the sound of her name, the dark-haired lady turned. "Do I know you?" She looked rather perplexed.

"We've not met officially," Ginger said. She held out a gloved hand. "I'm Mrs. Reed. My family and I have just registered here. I couldn't help but notice . . ." Ginger held her hand on her stomach, still flat. "I am as well. Is this your first?"

Mrs. Bainbridge blinked, and Ginger immediately became aware of her social faux pas, referring to the lady's condition so lightly. She'd stepped into American-level propriety, a consequence of all the years she'd spent in Boston, but something she hadn't done for quite some time. She began to apologise.

"I'm sorry—"

"No, it's quite all right. This is my second, so I'm

not nearly as sensitive about the topic, though my son is ten, so it's been a while."

"This is my first. I have an eleven-year-old son, but he's adopted, so this is new. Perhaps you would share your tips over tea sometime?" Ginger's request wasn't completely benign. She had a frightful curiosity and wanted to hear about the missing man, should Mrs. Bainbridge feel relief in talking about him, of course.

Mrs. Bainbridge answered haltingly. "Yes. Perhaps."

The attention of the entire foyer was suddenly captured by the sight of a very beautiful and glamorous blonde woman stepping down the staircase. With practised grace, the lady was clearly one used to commanding a room, and she had most definitely done that now.

Felicia moved to Ginger's side and whispered excitedly in her ear, "That's Poppy Kerslake!"

Miss Kerslake was a film star, and reports of her exploits dominated the society papers.

Mrs. Bainbridge laid eyes on the starlet, let out a stuttering sob, and then fled out of the front door of the hotel.

Ginger glanced over at Felicia. What kind of family drama had they stumbled into?

2

Ginger and Basil shared a spacious suite with their young son, and Boss, of course, whilst Felicia and Ambrosia shared a similar one next door. The rooms were a mix of Egyptian blue and mint green highlighted with gold trim and splashes of bright red. Linoleum floors were covered with large Persian rugs, and heavy, printed blue curtains hung from thick rods over tall windows.

"It's lovely," Ginger said.

The porter delivered the trunks, suitcases, and hat boxes to the appropriate rooms, and Lizzie joined Ginger to help her unpack. Ginger could imagine Langley getting to work helping Ambrosia with her things while the dowager carefully watched.

A tap on the door was followed by the soft-spoken voice of a woman dressed in a well-made, though plain, day frock which hung loosely over a remarkably thin frame.

"Good afternoon," she said. "Welcome to the Brighton Seaside Hotel. My name is Mrs. Merrick, and I'm the head housekeeper. Please let me know if there is anything you need, anything at all, during your stay, and I'll be sure to arrange it for you. We've many efficient chambermaids and porters on hand who are at your service."

Mrs. Merrick's gaze landed on Ginger, with a knowing look. Ginger surmised that the serious-faced woman was trained to attune herself immediately to the female in charge and waited for Ginger's reply. Ginger complied.

"Yes, thank you, Mrs. Merrick."

"I'll send the porter up to relieve you of your empty suitcases," Mrs. Merrick said. "We store them away for you until the time when you need them again."

"Thank you," Ginger said.

Mrs. Merrick stepped back. "Please ring if you find you require anything else."

As the housekeeper closed the door behind her, Ginger smiled at Basil. "I feel very well attended to."

Scout had his nose pressed against the window with Boss at his side, the dog's paws on the sill and his stubby tail shimmering. "Can we go to the beach after this?"

"If you like," Basil said. "I can take you swimming."

Scout faced Basil with a bashful look, "Oh, I don't know how to swim."

Basil grinned. "Then I shall teach you."

Ginger took a moment to study her reflection in the gold-framed mirror. She removed her high-top cloche hat, trimmed fashionably with a wide navy-blue ribbon, and ran her fingers through her red hair, cut short in a bob. Her green eyes were dull with fatigue, and her face was rather pale. She gently slapped her cheeks to encourage a bit of colour then claimed the blue chaise longue in the corner. Stretching out with a grateful sigh, Ginger said, "Lizzie, you're quite all right if I take a moment to rest?"

"Of course, madam. I've almost finished hanging your frocks and will take care of your hats and shoes next."

Basil insisted on unpacking his own suitcases and gave Scout instructions on doing the same. As each trunk and box was emptied, he and Scout moved them into the hall. "I hope they have a big storage room," Basil said with a smirk.

Ginger felt absolutely sluggardly and doubted she'd have the energy to go to the beach with her family that afternoon. Perhaps after a day's rest, she would feel more adventurous. She could at least rouse herself enough to venture down the corridor to check up on Felicia and Ambrosia.

Ginger tapped lightly on the slightly ajar door, and it pushed open. Felicia, her eyes bright with excitement, danced in a circle on the lemon-yellow carpet. "It's fabulous, Ginger!" She strolled to the window and with dramatic flair, pushed the net curtains apart. "The sea! I adore London, but the Thames pales next to the English Channel. Look at those colours!"

Ginger joined her sister-in-law and stared across the busy Kings Road—which going west turned into Kingsway and east, Marine Parade—and the drop down of the promenade to the pebbly beach ahead. The blue-green water of the Channel was certainly more appealing than the brown, muddy river they were accustomed to.

Felicia continued with unbridled excitement. "I can't wait to visit the shops!"

"Dear heavens," Ambrosia said, lowering herself into a blue velvet chair. "I'm tired out just from listening to you go on."

"Oh, Grandmama," Felicia said. "If you don't want to join us, Ginger and I can go alone."

"Please, do," Ambrosia said. "I rather fancy a lie-down." She turned her bulbous eyes to her maid. "Langley, have you almost finished?"

Langley dipped slightly at the knees, "Yes,

madam," then carried the last suitcase with her as she left the room.

"I think I'll change before we go," Felicia said.

"Felicia, darling," Ginger began, "I'm afraid I'm going to have to bow out as well and do as Grandmother is going to do."

"Oh blast, Ginger. Don't tell me I must go shopping alone?"

"I'll join you tomorrow," Ginger said. "I promise. I just need a day to recover from the exertion of the journey." Ginger placed a palm on her stomach as a reminder to Felicia that she had more than herself to think about.

"Fine. I'll simply browse today. Oh, perhaps I'll bump into Poppy Kerslake! How terribly wicked would it be if we became friends?"

Ginger let out a chuckle. "Miss Kerslake could do no better, I'm sure."

Leaving Ambrosia and Felicia to do what each must do to prepare for the afternoon, Ginger stepped into the corridor where she spotted Mrs. Bainbridge again. She lifted a hand to wave—after all, Ginger couldn't help her curiosity after the episode in the foyer with Miss Kerslake.

"Mrs. Bainbridge!"

The lady's head darted up, and she blinked on seeing Ginger. "Oh, hello again."

Ginger stepped towards Mrs. Bainbridge and smiled. "It seems we're neighbours."

"Yes, well, I'm afraid none of us on this floor will be good company. You have the misfortune of being grouped with the Bainbridge party. My brother-in-law, Austin, has been missing for over a week. You might have heard?"

"Yes, I'm sorry," Ginger said, her sympathy sincere. "I didn't know he was a relation."

"It was meant to be a happy holiday, and then Austin went for a swim one morning and didn't return. We don't have the heart to imagine the worst. We can't bear to leave until we know what happened."

"I see," Ginger said. "I imagine the police are investigating?"

Mrs. Bainbridge offered a vague smile. "They believe he drowned. Quentin, my husband, refuses to believe it." The lift bell rang, and the grated brass doors opened.

"Oh," Mrs. Bainbridge said when a young lad and a man stepped into the hallway. "This is my husband, Mr. Bainbridge, and my son, Reggie. Quentin, this is Mrs. Reed. Her family is visiting Brighton from London, on holiday for the week."

"A pleasure," Mr. Bainbridge said, then clearly not in the mood to chat, entered his room.

"Your son, Reggie, is similar in age to my son,

Scout," Ginger said. "Perhaps they can play together sometime."

"Perhaps," Mrs. Bainbridge said. "Now, if you would excuse me?"

"Of course," Ginger said. "Have a good day."

The door at the end of the corridor opened, and Miss Kerslake peeked out. She looked at Ginger in surprise then disappeared. For whom had she been looking?

Ginger pondered Mrs. Bainbridge's reaction to Miss Kerslake earlier and considered how awkward it must be for them both to be stationed on the same floor of the hotel. How very curious, indeed.

3

The next morning delivered another luxuriously beautiful day. After a good night's sleep and a simple but healthy breakfast of porridge and toast, Ginger felt fortified to face the day.

"The sea air is marvellous!" Ginger stated once they were stationed on the shore with their hired deckchairs and sun umbrellas.

She and Felicia had donned daring swimwear under their sundresses, swimming costumes that merely covered their torsos and ending with a loose-fitting tunic over tight shorts that ended at the knee. Ginger's outfit had bright blue and yellow vertical lines which she wore with a lemon-yellow swimming cap decorated with a daisy. Felicia's bathing tunic was a flattering pink trimmed with a silver neckline and matching belt that hung loosely at the hips. She had chosen a swimming hat in a contrasting jade green. Both ladies wore summer boots, suitable for a pebble beach. Ambrosia, fully dressed with a large hat on her grey head, sat upright in a deckchair beside them whilst Basil and Scout, also in torso-covering swimming costumes, frolicked in the water.

In the distance to the east, the pier jutted into the sea. Dotted all along the horizon, sailing boats and canoes rocked. Seabirds squawked overhead and a warm breeze billowed about, ruffling the hems of the ladies' sundresses. Other beachgoers joined them, more as the time ticked on, and soon the beach was rather crowded.

"I've failed to enquire about your shopping venture yesterday," Ginger said as she eyed Felicia from beyond the brim of her sun hat. "Did you befriend the lovely Miss Kerslake?"

Felicia lowered the book she'd made little effort to read. "The shops are lovely, and I'm afraid I couldn't resist picking up a few things—"

Ambrosia clucked her tongue. "We'll have to buy another carpetbag at this rate."

Felicia giggled, "Oh, Grandmama. I didn't see Miss Kerslake until I came back to my room. She stepped into the lift just after me, and I had to juggle my shopping bags to make room for us. She was rather unfriendly and actually looked down her nose on me!

It's at times like that that I wish I could rub in the fact that my late father was a *baron*."

"She doesn't seem the type to be impressed by titles," Ginger said, flipping a page of the latest fashion magazine issue of *La Femme Chic à Paris*.

"Everyone is impressed by titles," Ambrosia said tightly, "whether they admit it or not. Otherwise, the system would've broken down long ago."

Having once had a title, Ginger believed Ambrosia's statement had merit, at least in England. Ginger hadn't even used her title when she lived in Boston and only became known as Lady Gold after she'd moved back to her childhood home, Hartigan House, which she'd inherited from her father along with several profitable business ventures in '23. *Lady Gold* most certainly had more pull in London society than Mrs. Reed, but Ginger had never for a second regretted her marriage to Basil Reed.

Her gaze sought him out, and she smiled at her good fortune. Basil Reed, wearing his swimming costume, was a sight to behold. Ginger was familiar with his well-built form, but, oh mercy, she'd never seen so much of it on display for the public to see.

As if he could sense she was staring at him, he glanced over and smiled. Droplets of seawater damp-ened his hair, and he shook his head to set them free, a move that made Ginger's heart skip a beat. *How handsome he is!*

Scout grabbed Basil's hand as they returned to the empty chairs in their circle, with little Boss happily kicking up pebbles in their wake. Ambrosia pushed her weight to the edge of her chair. "Langley!"

Her maid, who waited with Lizzie under the shade of a sun umbrella close by, hurried to her mistress and assisted her to her feet.

"Please take me to my room."

"Poor Grandmama," Felicia said as they watched the older lady leave. "I fear the amount of skin on display has offended her sensibilities." As if to emphasise her point, Felicia crossed a bare leg.

Ginger didn't want to admit that she wasn't feeling in tip-top shape either, so she was relieved when Felicia gathered her things.

"Are you going in already?" Ginger asked.

"I spotted a lovely frock in a shop window yesterday that I regret not trying on. Would you like to come with me to see it?"

Ginger was jolly keen on fashion, and even an upset tummy wouldn't keep her from joining Felicia if she could help it. "I'd love to," she said. "Basil darling, are you staying?"

"Please, Dad?" Scout said. "I don't want to leave yet."

"We can stay a little longer, son," Basil said, "but then we must go in for lunch."

Ginger laughed at Scout's eagerness to play. After so many years living on the streets of London and often fending for himself, Scout had missed out on playing and enjoying being a child. Ginger was pleased that he was having fun.

Basil got to his feet, which were bare and red from the cold water. "How would you ladies like to go out on a sailing boat this afternoon? They're available to hire."

"I didn't know you knew how to sail, love," Ginger said.

"Not expertly, no," Basil said. "We'll engage a captain."

Ginger shared a look with Felicia, who nodded her chin. "We could go to the shop afterwards, I suppose?"

"I mean, we can shop anytime in London," Felicia added, "but sailing in the Channel isn't an opportunity that comes around all the time."

Ginger smiled at Basil. "It looks like sailing it is!"

"Jolly good." Basil turned to Scout, "Let's go and make reservations, and then later we can get fish and chips from the beach vendor."

Ginger loved sailing, and while living in Boston, she had had plenty of opportunities. She prayed that her stomach tumbles would settle enough by later in the day. Most afternoons, they usually did, and all she would need was a short rest beforehand.

Linking arms, Ginger and Felicia strolled along the promenade and up the steps to Kings Road before carefully crossing it and entering the hotel.

It took a moment for their eyes to adjust to the dimmer lighting after the brightness of the mid-morning sun. A light-haired, blue-eyed gentleman in a pinstriped suit with a single-breasted jacket, slender black tie, and loose-fitting pleated trousers cuffed at the ankles, tipped his hat as he strolled by.

Watching the man until he left the hotel, Felicia grasped Ginger's arm. "Ginger, do you believe in love at first sight?"

"Not again," Ginger said playfully. "You're always falling for men you don't know."

"But there's something about his eyes," Felicia said dreamily. "I really believe we were meant to meet."

Ginger failed to share Felicia's enthusiasm. There was something about the gentleman's eyes—a brief flicker of recognition passed through them when he saw her. Ginger couldn't place just where, but she was certain that she *had* met the man before.

4

*B*efore walking along the seafront with Scout towards the boats-for-hire hut, Basil took a moment to slip on his loose sailor-style beach trousers and matching shirt, which took a bit of finesse as his swimming costume was still damp. He mused at the flexibility of human propriety as he scanned the shoreline. The skin on display would make the sunbathers redden in dismay and judgement if a similar standard was worn anywhere else, other than a few feet from open water. Basil could barely believe what he was currently wearing in public.

For a gentleman of his years, recently turned forty-three, he still caught the fancy of women of all ages. Even as he strolled along the beach, he felt the female gazes, followed by titters of whispering with their companions.

Despite Basil being apparently intriguing to the opposite sex, he was the loyal type. Since almost losing the opportunity to spend his life with Ginger, he never took her presence at his side for granted. Not only would he never risk a dalliance that might end up with him hurting Ginger, he also wasn't even tempted. Ginger was everything he'd ever wanted in a woman. She was beautiful and kind, intelligent and wise, charming and courageous. She'd saved his life on more than one occasion.

He worried about her now, with a child growing, and how ill she'd been over the last few weeks. Basil was unused to seeing his wife in any state of weakness; however, her physician had reassured them that stomach upset in the early weeks was quite normal.

Her condition was a blessing that had come as a complete shock. Basil's first wife, now deceased, had never wanted children. Basil hadn't realised that she'd taken matters into her own hands without telling him, and when children didn't come, he accepted that being a father wasn't part of God's plan for his life.

Then he had married Ginger, a decade his junior, but this time, nature was against them. Ginger had longed to be a mother, but despite her desires, it appeared this would not be something they would be granted. It hadn't happened with her first husband, so she wasn't surprised when children didn't quickly come for her and Basil either. Fortunately, Scout had come into their lives, and adopting him had made them happy parents.

Basil watched as Scout ran ahead and chuckled at how little the pebbly beach seemed to impact the soles of the young lad's feet. Used to the comfort of socks and shoes, Basil walked warily and occasionally winced when happening upon a rough stone. Bringing Scout to Brighton had been a good idea. The lad was small for his age, and Basil worried about his thin frame.

His son stopped ahead, having encountered another lad, dressed more soberly than attire at the beach required. This didn't stop the boy from picking up a piece of driftwood and throwing it into the sea. Boss barked and started after it. Scout called him back, and Basil continued to be amazed at how obedient the small dog remained.

When he reached the boys, Basil smiled at them then asked Scout, "Who's your new friend?"

"This is Reggie," Scout answered. "He's staying at the same hotel as us!"

"Nice to meet you, Reggie. Where's your mother?"

"She's not feeling well. My dad is going to take me out on a sailing boat."

Basil's gaze went to the gentleman who'd arrived at the boat-rental hut before Basil had got there. He also wore a suit and hat not intended for wear on the beach.

Basil stepped up behind him. "Lovely day for a sail," he said.

The man turned. "There's only a medium-size craft available for this afternoon. Too large for just my son and me. He'll be disappointed."

Basil looked back at Scout, who displayed a big-toothed grin. It was then that he realised Scout had very few friends his age. A quick stab of emotion hit the target.

"There's four in my sailing party," Basil said. Ginger, Scout, and Felicia had their hearts set on sailing that afternoon. Ambrosia had made it clear she wasn't about to set foot on anything that didn't remain firmly under foot.

"You and your son are welcome to join us," Basil continued. "It appears our children have made friends."

"That's very kind of you," the man said. "Normally, I'd book a smaller one for tomorrow, but alas, I feel it's time my family and I leave Brighton." He held out a hand. "Bainbridge. You've met my son, Reggie."

"Reed," Basil returned. "My deepest sympathies on the loss of your brother."

"Thank you. After surviving the war, he dies whilst on holiday. Such a tragedy." Bainbridge shifted his shoulders back and exhaled. "Everyone has lost somebody. We must all move on."

"Indeed, we must."

BASIL DISCUSSED the terms with the captain of the sailing boat.

"Two hours and a lovely time, I assure you," the jolly man said. He wore a white sailor's cap on a head fringed with white hair. The leathery lines on his face betrayed an age of days exposed to the sun and wind. His eyes twinkled, almost disappearing when he smiled. "It's all the peace and relaxing you'll need."

"Sounds delightful," Basil said. He turned to address Bainbridge. "Are you sure there's no one else from your party who'd like to join us?"

"Mrs. Bainbridge is incapacitated at the moment. I didn't even want her to come to Brighton, but she insisted. I fear she's paying for her stubbornness now. Her feet are so swollen, well . . ." He paused as if recognising he'd probably shared too much. "Perhaps Lord Davenport-Witt would like to join. He's the Earl of Wincanton, a dear friend of Austin's. I believe he tolerates that Findley." He frowned. "I'm not dreadfully fond of him myself."

Basil wasn't aware of either man, and didn't feel

the need to enquire more deeply into Bainbridge's affairs.

"Very well. I'm returning with Scout to the hotel to change. Are you headed that way?"

"I think I'll linger a little longer. Reggie and I will meet you back here later."

Basil dipped his chin then called for Scout and Boss, the former showing fresh excitement on learning that his new friend would join them later.

Scooping Boss under one arm and taking Scout's hand with the other, Basil safely led them across the busy Kings Road. Glancing up at the second floor of the hotel, he saw Felicia in the window. She smiled when she spotted them and waved.

5

The entire time in the lift, Ginger and Felicia discussed love at first sight.

"One can hardly be in love with a man when one doesn't know a fig about him," Ginger insisted. "For heaven's sake, Felicia, you don't even know the gentleman's name."

"You saw the way he looked at me. Eyes as deep blue as the sea, brooding desire, the current of electricity that shot between us—"

Ginger laughed out loud. "You've been reading too many penny dreadfuls." She snatched the book tucked under Felicia's arm and read the title, *Women in Love*.

"It's not a penny dreadful!" Felicia snatched back the novel written by D. H. Lawrence and held it to her heart. "Laugh if you must, but I know in the depths of my soul, that he's the one for me."

"I do hope the fellow is single," Ginger said. *And that Ambrosia would approve*, though Ginger kept that thought to herself. Felicia was beyond caring if her choice of gentleman *du jour* pleased her grandmother, and her ongoing single status was a point of contention between the two Gold women.

When they reached their floor, the lift attendant opened the gate. Ginger had to give the man credit for holding in the grin that balanced on the edge of his smile.

"Thank you, Mr. Weaver."

Ginger and Felicia paused at their respective doors. "One hour?" Felicia said.

"Let's eat before we go. Basil and Scout aren't coming in for lunch, so I'll order something to be brought up. We'll take it in your suite so Ambrosia can join us."

Having their luxurious room to herself was what Ginger needed at that moment. Setting her beach bag on the table, she found herself drawn to the chaise longue. *I'll lie down for a few minutes before deciding on an outfit suitable for sailing. I should ring for Lizzie—*

The next thing she knew, Ginger was startled awake by loud knocking on the door. She checked her watch. *Oh mercy.* An hour had passed, and she'd slept through it! Hurrying to the door, she opened it to Felicia, whose countenance soured.

"You're not dressed. Did you order lunch?"

"I fell asleep." Ginger's hand went to her belly. "I can't believe how this one, barely the size of a plum, drains all my energy. What will I do when it becomes full size?"

Felicia smiled, her eyes softening with forgiveness. "I'll order lunch, but you must hurry. I just looked out of the window and saw Basil and Scout heading this way."

The lift bell rang, and Ginger thought it was indicative of her husband and son's arrival.

Felicia tugged on Ginger's arm, unceremoniously pulling her into the corridor. The gentleman who'd so quickly captured Felicia's heart had stepped into view, along with a second shorter man. When the gentlemen spotted them, the one who'd caught Felicia's eye said, "Good day, ladies. I hope you're enjoying your visit to Brighton." Of the two, he was the more attractive and apparently less reserved than his companion who stayed quiet.

Felicia giggled and patted at her short, dark finger waves. She'd changed into a yellow summer frock of printed georgette with a one-side jabot and a showy bow on the girdle sash. She looked fresh and youthful. Still in her beach clothes, Ginger felt tired and haggard in comparison, a feeling she was most definitely not used to.

"We just arrived yesterday," Felicia said. "Today has been lovely so far."

"Are you with the Bainbridge party?" Ginger asked. Mrs. Bainbridge had mentioned that the rest of the floor had been reserved for them. When the men nodded, she added, "I'm so sorry to hear about your missing friend. Still no word?"

"Thank you, madam," the short one said. "I'm afraid we've not had any promising news."

Removing his hat, the taller man said, "Please forgive my manners. I'm Davenport-Witt, and this is Findley."

Mr. Findley removed his hat. "How do you do?"

Felicia answered for them both, "Very well, thank you."

Davenport-Witt. Where had Ginger heard that name before?

"Charles is being modest," Mr. Findley added smoothly. "He's the Earl of Wincanton and calls himself Lord Davenport-Witt."

Ginger scanned Lord Davenport-Witt's features and a memory formed. The casual suit became a soldier's uniform, the face thinner, and the blue eyes more youthful.

"Where did you serve during the war, Lord Davenport-Witt?" Ginger asked.

The man smiled. "France, as did many an Englishman."

"It's only that you look familiar. Oh, now, it's me with poor manners. I'm Mrs. Reed. This is my sister-in-law, Miss Gold."

The gentlemen took the ladies' hands in turn, but Lord Davenport-Witt held on to Felicia's palm. "Gold? Are you a relative of Daniel, Lord Gold?"

Felicia blushed as she withdrew her hand. "Daniel was my brother."

"And my first husband," Ginger added.

Lord Davenport-Witt's eyes flashed with surprise. "You're Lady Gold?"

"Formerly." Ginger still used the handle Lady Gold when she worked as a private investigator or in consultation with Scotland Yard. Not only did the title give her better access when probing for answers, but it also helped her and Basil avoid introducing themselves as husband and wife when on a case together. She added, "I'm afraid my late husband never mentioned you to me."

Daniel had never mentioned Lord Davenport-Witt, but Ginger had most definitely heard of him. Her work with the British secret service had brought much-classified information her way. Something about her memory of him, or lack of, niggled at the back of her mind. Whatever it was, she felt a sense of caution.

Lord Davenport-Witt let out a short breath, and Ginger detected a sense of relief at her apparent lack of knowledge. Whatever he was hiding, he wanted to keep a secret.

"You knew my dear brother," Felicia said, her hands clasped at her heart. "You must tell me everything. I have so little of him to remember."

"I would be delighted to regale you, Miss Gold. Perhaps you will join Findley and me for dinner tonight?" He glanced at Ginger. "You and Mr. Reed are welcome to join us, of course."

"You're very kind," Ginger said, "though we have plans to go sailing, so I'm not sure when we will be available. Perhaps you should make plans for tomorrow night, Felicia?"

Felicia let out a soft sigh. "I suppose, if you'll still be here, Lord Davenport-Witt?"

Mr. Findley shuffled his weight with a look of impatience. Ginger would guess that the plainer-looking fellow was used to being overlooked and inconvenienced. The phenomenon of being overshadowed by a more attractive, more vivacious personality in the room wasn't reserved for the gentler sex alone.

Before a new arrangement could be made, the last door down the hall opened, and the very phenomenon

Ginger had been pondering happened. Poppy Kerslake radiated glamour with shiny blonde-bobbed hair, perfectly Marcelled and clipped off a wide forehead with a hairpin made of pearls. Her flawless skin was made up with bright-red lipstick, round pink cheeks, and arched eyebrows plucked to a thin line. She wore a sophisticated blue tunic frock in Mongolian crepe with a satin-flounced collar and cuffs.

The starlet gave Ginger and Felicia a cursory glance as she elegantly strolled to Lord Davenport-Witt's side.

"Charles, darling?" Miss Kerslake's purr had a distinctive Australian accent. She wiggled long fingers, bare but for a striking opal ring, the large gem glittering with hues of pinks, greens, and blues in the electric lights of the corridor sconces. She linked her bare arm with Lord Davenport-Witt's, subtly marking her territory. "Are we ready to go?"

Lord Davenport-Witt returned his hat to his head, and Mr. Findley, a second behind, did the same.

"It was a pleasure meeting you both," the earl said, his smile strained, then stepped in stride with Miss Kerslake towards the lift. Miss Kerslake shot a quick look over her shoulder, her eyes narrowing on Felicia as if casting a warning. Lord Davenport-Witt placed a hand on the starlet's back, guiding her into the lift, then stepped in behind her, Mr. Findley following.

The lift doors closed, and Felicia grunted. "That minx!"

Ginger felt a wave of pity. "I'm afraid you've got your work cut out for you, love."

Felica huffed, spun on the heels of her T-strap shoes, and marched down the plush carpet runner of the hotel corridor.

6

"It turns out that Mr. Bainbridge and young Reggie will join us," Basil said. Since he and Scout had already eaten, he drank tea as the others enjoyed luncheon. "It's a numbers thing."

Ginger lowered her fork. "Mrs. Bainbridge is rather large with child, so I can understand why she wouldn't want to come."

"I offered for him to bring other members of his party, but he was quite reluctant, except for a Lord Davenport-Witt."

Felicia tipped her wine glass, spilling a drop on the tablecloth at the sound of the earl's name.

"Child," Ambrosia said. "You're rather clumsy today. What's got into you?"

Basil caught the look shared by Ginger and Felicia and wondered what he and Ambrosia were missing.

"Butterfingers," Felicia said. "That is all." Then without looking at Basil, she added, "Do you know if the earl will be joining us?"

The corner of Basil's mouth twitched as understanding dawned. At some point, Felicia had become acquainted with the earl and was clearly taken by the man. Dear Felicia was always infatuated with one fellow or another, much to Ambrosia's consternation. Surely, the Dowager Lady Gold would be pleased that her granddaughter was finally interested in a man with a title, and by the way the elderly lady's blue eyes latched on to her granddaughter, she'd caught the nuance of Felicia's question too.

"An earl is staying at this hotel?" she said. "Why have I not been notified? We should've been introduced."

"We've only just found out about the earl ourselves," Ginger said. "Felicia and I ran into Lord Davenport-Witt and his friend, Mr. Findley, in the corridor when we returned from the beach."

Ambrosia placed a well-jewelled, wrinkled hand over Felicia's. "A good possibility."

Despite an obvious interest in this person, Felicia couldn't keep from protesting. "Grandmama!"

Ginger broke in. "We're uncertain that the earl is available for romantic pursuits. It appears that he has been spoken for."

"Oh," Ambrosia said. "By whom?"

"Miss Poppy Kerslake," Felicia said sourly.

"And who is Miss Kerslake in society?" Ambrosia asked. "I've never heard of her."

"She's a starlet," Ginger replied. "She's in many popular motion pictures."

Ambrosia waved her hand. "Pfft. An earl would never marry an actress." She steadied her eyes on Basil. "You must invite Lord Davenport-Witt on your little excursion." She rose to her feet with the energy and determination of someone much younger than her eighty years. "Ring the bell for the porter to come to my room. I'll have him deliver the note straight away."

UNFORTUNATELY, as the weather in coastal regions was wont to do, the wind picked up from the south-west that afternoon to create undesirable sailing conditions.

"Oh bother," Ginger said. Her eyes darted to the second bedroom of the suite where Scout was quietly reading. "And Scout was so looking forward to it. I hate to disappoint him."

Before Basil could respond, a knock on the door interrupted them.

"Oh hello, Bainbridge," Basil said, opening the door.

In the sitting area, Ginger craned her neck to see a portion of Quentin Bainbridge's form along with young Reggie.

"I hate to interrupt you, Mr. Reed," Mr. Bainbridge said, "but I imagine you've seen the state of the Channel out of your windows."

"Indeed. I fear we'll have to postpone our outing until tomorrow and hope for calmer seas."

"Young Reggie is dreadfully disappointed, and to appease him, I've promised a trip to the aquarium. Reggie would very much like it if Scout came along."

Ginger watched Reggie's expression, which remained staid, neither proving nor disproving his father's statement.

"I think Scout would be delighted."

Scout, having heard the knock and his name mentioned, was found hovering by his doorway. "I would, Dad. I can go, can't I?"

Ginger felt mixed about the offer. She wanted to take Scout to the aquarium herself, but she couldn't deny how happy he looked to spend time with his new friend. She and Basil could take him another time, Ginger supposed. Youths never tired of seeing sea creatures up close.

"It's fine with me," Ginger said.

"Off you go then," Basil added with a smile.

Basil tucked a bit of money in Scout's pocket and

sent him on his way. He turned to Ginger with a raised brow. "How would you like to spend your afternoon?"

"I'm frightfully put off by the prospect of lounging about all the time. I'm sleeping away my days. Please, Basil, take me away from this couch!"

Basil lowered himself into one of the chairs. "There's plenty to see and do in Brighton that doesn't involve the seaside."

"Oh, I know," Ginger said. "Let's go to the Royal Pavilion. I've heard it's quite a wonder."

Ginger sparked the interest of Ambrosia and Felicia, and soon, the foursome exited a taxicab a few streets north of the Brighton Marine Palace and Pier, in front of the majestic Royal Pavilion, a multi-domed structure with many spires, arches, and decorative features.

Felicia was sufficiently awed. "It looks like it was magically transported here from India!"

Briefly, the sun's rays poked through a mass of clouds to create the illusion that the palace had been made of gold.

Ambrosia's walking stick tapped against the concrete, and Ginger smiled as Felicia immediately stepped beside her grandmother and gave her a supportive arm. Felicia and Ginger's late husband, Daniel, had lost both their parents in a carriage accident when they were children. Ambrosia, already a widow, had stepped in to raise the siblings. Daniel was already a teenager at the time, but Felicia was a young, impressionable girl. Despite Ambrosia's prickly persona and dated Victorian views, she loved Felicia ferociously and wanted the best for her. Felicia rebelled incessantly, and the fact that her antics hadn't put Ambrosia into an early grave was a testament to the fortitude the Dowager Lady Gold possessed.

"I don't like the wind," Ambrosia stated. "Far too windy in the coastal regions. I prefer Bray Manor in Chesterton, but London does in a push."

Certainly, there was no wind inside the palace, but the interior took one's breath away, none the less. Room after extravagant room was outmatched by the richly decorated banqueting room. A delightful palette of lemon yellow, lime green, apple red, and deep sky blue, the carpets ran wall to wall. Woven tapestries hung from ceiling to floor and decadent red draperies, trimmed in gold, flounced above long, church-style windows. Several jewel-encrusted crystal chandeliers hung from the painted ceilings, the king among them from the centre of the room, which dropped from a mural of palm branches against a vivid blue dome.

"Such opulence," Ambrosia said. "I would say the young king outdid himself."

"He started building when he was the Prince of Wales, and later as Prince Regent," Basil explained.

Though Ginger was thoroughly English—born in London—from the age of eight, she had been raised in Boston, Massachusetts, and had missed out on the finer points of monarchical history.

However, she was aware of the more recent historical points of interest. "It's hard to believe that this palace was used as a field hospital." Ginger stared at the large photographs of injured men, in beds, row after row, with a large chandelier hanging incongruously from the ornate, domed ceiling above.

It wasn't difficult to spend an hour or two gawking at the painted ceilings and lavish furnishings—the palace was well occupied by others with the same idea. Ginger grew fatigued, and Basil seemed to notice.

"Are you ready to go back to the hotel?" he asked.

"Quite," Ginger replied.

Felicia stepped quickly to Ginger's side. "Over there."

Perplexed by Felicia's tense demeanour, Ginger followed her gaze. Understanding fell when she spotted Lord Davenport-Witt with Miss Kerslake at his side, and she explained the significance to Basil.

"They don't look that bothered by the fact that a friend of theirs is unaccounted for," Basil said.

As if he could feel he was being watched and talked about, the earl stepped in their direction, his eyes lighting with recognition when he saw them.

"Oh, hello," he called out.

Poppy Kerslake looked none too delighted, and Ginger could see the flash of warning in her eyes when her gaze landed on Felicia. Felicia, never one to be intimidated, smiled brightly in return.

"Lord Davenport-Witt, Miss Kerslake, what a surprise!"

"One must do something to keep amused," Miss Kerslake said.

"I suppose it is rather difficult," Felicia concurred, "when one's good friend is missing and presumed to have encountered misfortune."

Ginger hissed in her sister-in-law's ear. "Felicia!"

The corner of the earl's lip tugged slowly upwards. "It's true; our holiday time has taken a sour turn. I hope yours is better, Miss Gold?"

"Delightful so far. Tomorrow we're going sailing. We would be out there right now, if not for the weather. Do you sail, Lord Davenport-Witt?"

"Not as much as I'd like."

Ginger glanced at Basil. Was it just her or had everyone, but the earl and Felicia, disappeared from the room? Miss Kerslake's cheeks were red with umbrage, while Ambrosia looked as if she'd burst with delight. It was such a rare emotion to witness that Ginger felt like she'd stepped into the pages of her book.

Basil cleared his throat. "It's been a pleasure to meet you both, but we were just about to head back to the hotel."

"I'm sure we'll bump into each other again," Lord Davenport-Witt said.

The taxicab ride was nearly unbearable with Felicia and Ambrosia, uncharacteristically in agreement, singing the earl's praises all the way back to the hotel.

7

*T*he next day turned out to be perfect for sailing. A short taxicab ride delivered them to the jetty where a forty-four-foot wooden sailing boat awaited them. It had two masts, three sails, and was edged with varnished teak benches.

"'Ad to store 'er inland during the war," the captain said, "but since then, I've polished 'er up and take 'er out whenever I can."

"She's a beauty," Basil replied.

"Indeed, she is," the captain's face beamed with pride. "I said to the missus, gotta share the joy with visitors like you, eh? Can't be 'oggin' 'er all to myself."

With light-hearted anticipation, Basil, Ginger, Scout, and Felicia, along with Quentin Bainbridge, his son, Reggie, and Lord Davenport-Witt, boarded the vessel.

Scout and Reggie leaned over the starboard side of the sailing boat and giggled as they ran their fingers through the wake. And the light breeze kept the occupants cool and in motion.

Ginger, with Boss on her lap, and Felicia sat in the stern of the vessel—the latter with her eyes continually darting to the earl—whilst the men smoked at the bow. Basil could see the appeal. The earl was tall, confident, and a rather worthy seaman himself. He produced a package of cigars, offering it to Basil and Quentin Bainbridge. "Cigar, gentlemen?"

Basil, who smoked on rare occasions, thought this one was as good a time as any. "Yes, thank you, old chap."

Basil had also arranged for champagne to be brought aboard, and the captain made a show of dispatching the bottle cap with a loud pop and pouring the bubbly liquid into flat coupé glasses.

"Ladies first," he said with a toothy grin.

Ginger, choosing a simple tonic water, along with Felicia, accepted their drinks with grace and gratitude.

"Thank you, Captain!"

When an appropriate amount of time had passed, Davenport-Witt excused himself. "I mustn't be rude by ignoring the beautiful ladies on board. You don't mind, Reed, do you?"

"I'm sure they'd be delighted with your company,"

Basil said. When the earl was out of earshot, he muttered to Bainbridge. "Is he a rogue?"

Bainbridge tapped ashes over the side of the vessel. "I honestly don't know the chap all that well. Carries himself with a bit of mystery. So very vague when asked a direct question, especially about how he spent his time during the Great War."

"Adeline, my wife, is quite enamoured of him, as are all the ladies, but I can't begrudge her any diversion now. The poor dear is terribly uncomfortable." He added rather uncharitably, "Like a human pear with legs."

Basil watched his wife and Felicia as they engaged in conversation with the earl. Felicia was flushed with giddiness, certainly not hiding her flirtatious efforts. Ginger listened in with the aloofness of a chaperone trying desperately not to be a gooseberry in the group of three, and considered the gentleman politely. Her green eyes studied the man with interest, but there was a look in them that someone who didn't know his wife as he did mightn't recognise—distrust.

But why? Ginger was normally so inclusive and the first to give a stranger the benefit of the doubt. What was it about the earl that troubled his astute wife?

8

*G*inger wished there was a dial on Felicia's back so that she could turn her sister-in-law's flirtatious enthusiasm down a notch. By Ginger's judgement, it was apparent that the intrigue ran both ways; the earl could hardly keep his eyes off Felicia and her lovely smile as she giggled.

However, Miss Kerslake was still an unknown in this equation, and Ginger would hate for Felicia's heart to be wounded. In all seriousness, with her poor history choosing men, one would think she would have learned her lesson by now and proceed with caution.

Felicia, one bare arm folded over her chest and the other propping her glass in the air, said lightly, "Lord Davenport-Witt, you were going to tell me about my brother?"

"Ah yes." The earl shifted his weight, his blue eyes

moving upward as he seemed to draw on his memories. "Gold was a good old chap, wasn't he? Always had a kind word to say about his fellow man. And dreadfully good at cards. Lost a dozen or so cigarettes in the trenches to him myself."

Ginger felt a strange wave of nostalgia course through her veins. It'd been so long since she'd spoken to someone, other than Felicia and Ambrosia, who'd known Daniel personally. She loved Basil dearly and the life they now had together, but Daniel had been her first love and losing him to the war had been so difficult.

"When was the last time you saw him?" she asked.

"Oh blast, summer of eighteen, I believe. Somewhere in France."

Ginger smiled weakly. "Were you in his regiment?"

"No, we weren't in the same regiment, but our regiments did cross paths on occasion. We were both stationed near Brussels for a few weeks. Gold and I got on well—as if we'd known each other our whole lives. I was very sorry to hear when his regiment was lost."

Felicia murmured. "It was a sad day for all of us."

Ginger stayed quiet. She wanted to believe Lord Davenport-Witt, and she had no logical reason not to, except something about the earl's demeanour didn't sit quite right with her. She couldn't put her finger on it—for one thing, Daniel had never been one to play cards, much less win at them. She supposed he could've picked it up during the war years, and she would never have known, though she just couldn't picture it. The Daniel she knew never gambled. His family had lost its fortune because of a gambling addiction by both Daniel's father and grandfather. And Daniel had vowed never to tempt fate.

However, the war had had a way of changing the hearts and minds of many faithful and determined folk.

Ginger felt a tug on her summer frock and glanced down at Scout, his face scrunched in an adorable, childlike manner, his skinny arm outstretched, and finger pointed.

"Something just bobbed up in the water, Mum. Reggie thought it was a whale, but it's got no spout."

Ginger shielded her eyes from the sun's glare on the water and stared in the direction her son pointed. His announcement had the attention of all the passengers and the captain included, everyone eyeing the large object floating nearby.

Basil shouted, "Take us closer, Captain!"

As they drew near, Ginger could make out its rectangular shape. A trunk? The bubbles appearing around it made the inanimate object look like it was breathing.

The sight of it made Ginger's heart slow.

Quickly she went to Basil's side and whispered in his ear. "It appears as if gas is being released."

Her husband nodded sombrely and whispered back. "A body?"

Ginger's dear pathologist friend, Haley Higgins, who'd spent a couple of years living with Ginger while attending the London Medical School for Women, had explained the process one evening over a glass of brandy. Tiny microbes eat away at the corpse, releasing gas while reducing the body's density. Over time, the result will be that a body submerged in water will find its way to the surface.

"Only one way to find out," she said.

Basil instructed the captain again. "Can we bring it aboard?"

Aligning the vessel with the trunk, Basil and the earl reached for one end, whilst Mr. Bainbridge and the captain reached for the other. Ginger, Felicia, and the boys stood on the opposite side of the boat to help distribute the weight, but the men plus the heavy trunk caused the sailing boat to lurch towards the port side.

"Hang on!" Ginger yelled, gripping the railing with both hands. Felicia, Scout, and Reggie did the same. Boss yelped as he slid to a spot behind her legs.

"It's okay, Bossy," Ginger said, hoping everyone aboard could swim. At least Scout and Reggie wore life jackets.

"Heave ho!" the captain shouted, and with loud grunts accompanying great exertion, the trunk was lifted onto the boat. The men spread out, which brought the vessel back to balance.

"Treasure," the captain said with a grin.

Basil didn't return the smile. "I'm afraid treasure wouldn't float to the surface."

"What is it then?" Mr. Bainbridge said.

Ginger held Basil's gaze and then let her eyes float to Scout and Reggie. It wouldn't do to open the trunk with them as witnesses.

"We can't know until we open it," Basil said, "but let's get it to shore first, shall we?"

Ginger noticed that the earl had grown quiet, and if she wasn't mistaken, the man demonstrated slight hints of agitation.

"Are you all right, Lord Davenport-Witt?" she asked.

He blinked as he stared back at her. "I recognise the trunk."

It was a classic Vuittonite trunk by Louis Vuitton made of orange-stained, water-resistant canvas. Ginger had a similar one herself.

"It belongs to Miss Kerslake," he explained. "It went missing a week ago."

9

Once the ladies and children were safely on shore, Ginger asked Felicia to take the boys back to the hotel. Felicia shot her a questioning look—a look of not wanting to miss the action, or, more specifically, the *earl* in action. Still, when Ginger whispered her suspicions, Felicia was glad to comply.

Ginger stood aside as the men carried the heavy trunk off the plank, unable to avoid getting the bottoms of their trousers and their footwear soaked.

Mr. Bainbridge wiped the sweat from his brow, his eyebrows nearly meeting above his nose as he questioned the others. "What's this then?"

Basil shared a look with Ginger before unbuckling the straps. A rusted locking apparatus didn't budge.

"Captain, a tool, perhaps?"

"Aye, I've got a kit on board. A screwdriver should do it."

Moments later, the captain returned with the instrument in hand and gave it to Basil, who worked the lock until it broke off. Basil glanced up at Mr. Bainbridge and Lord Davenport-Witt. "Gentlemen, prepare yourselves."

The lid flew open, and a gasp escaped the mouths of all the onlookers. As Ginger had predicted, a body in a forced foetal position lay inside. The corpse was bloated with skin shedding like a snake, and the facial features were deformed, possibly nibbled on by various sea creatures. It was clear, however, that the deceased was male with dirty-blond hair.

Ginger felt bile rise in her throat. Normally, she was as solid as a rock when viewing gruesome remains —she'd seen plenty during the war. She blamed her queasiness on her "delicate" condition. It didn't help when Mr. Bainbridge turned his back to the chest and vomited on the pebbled beach.

Oh mercy.

Lord Davenport-Witt spoke grimly. "It's his brother, Austin."

Basil commanded the captain to fetch the police. To Bainbridge, who'd recovered and had washed his face with seawater, and to Lord Davenport-Witt, he said, "In full disclosure, I'm Chief Inspector Basil Reed of Scotland Yard. I'm afraid your brother's no longer a missing person case, Mr. Bainbridge. This is murder."

Mr. Bainbridge's knees bent weakly, and Lord Davenport-Witt stepped over to brace him in time to prevent an ungraceful fall. "There, there, old chap. Hang on to me."

"You believe this trunk belongs to Poppy Kerslake, Lord Davenport-Witt?" Ginger said. "Why is that?"

"The Australian flag is emblazoned on one side."

Ginger pursed her lips. "How is it that you are so well acquainted with Miss Kerslake's luggage?"

Lord Davenport-Witt blinked, and as Ginger suspected, was too much of a gentleman to kiss and tell. "Miss Kerslake was hot and bothered when the porter couldn't produce her trunk at her request. She presented a very clear description of it to us all and had all the staff of the hotel searching high and low, including the manager and chief housekeeper—the same ones in employment at the hotel now. They, of course, were full of apologies, claiming to have no idea what could have happened to Miss Kerslake's trunk. They tag every piece of luggage then stow it in the luggage room with the owner's name, in and out dates, and room numbers."

Ginger thought the earl's answer to her question was overly thorough but kept her feelings on that to herself.

The captain jogged back to them, his face red from the effort, and tried without success to conceal his shortness of breath. Ginger gathered running along the seafront wasn't a pastime he normally engaged in if he spent most of his time sailing the Channel.

"The police are on their way," he finally stated.

AFTER WHAT FELT LIKE EONS, a police motor car puttered to the kerb on Kingsway, and two officers dressed in dark navy-blue uniforms with single-breasted jackets and police helmets jumped out.

Such heavy clothes in the summer heat, Ginger thought, feeling sorry for them.

Basil was quick to introduce himself.

"Pleased to meet you, Chief Inspector," the older of the two officers said. "This is Constable James Clarke, and I'm Detective Inspector William Attwood. I've been leading the case of Mr. Austin Bainbridge's disappearance. When the call came in, I wondered . . ."

"We have identification for Austin Bainbridge," Basil said. He lifted his chin towards Quentin Bainbridge. "This is his brother, Mr. Quentin Bainbridge, and family friend, Lord Davenport-Witt."

Detective Inspector Attwood removed his helmet. "Of course. I'm sorry to see you both again in such sad circumstances. My condolences on this unhappy discovery." His eyes landed on Ginger, and as she was highly accustomed to, he frowned at the presence of a lady at the site of such gruesomeness. Ginger had had plenty of experience with death—first during the Great War, then as a consultant for Scotland Yard, and lately, her work as a private investigator. She normally had a strong stomach for wretched sights and smells.

Ginger held out her hand. "I'm Mrs. Reed."

"Pleased to meet you, madam. I do believe we have things handled here. Do you need an escort to your room?"

Basil interrupted. "What you don't know about my wife, Detective Inspector Attwood, is that she's a private investigator and often works as a consultant for Scotland Yard."

Detective Inspector Attwood didn't seem too keen to hear the news, but Lord Davenport-Witt let out a whistle. "A lady investigator! Impressive!"

Detective Inspector Attwood turned to his assisting officer. "Constable Clarke, call the medical examiner and an ambulance."

The police presence on the beach had triggered the interest of other holidaymakers, but with the trunk lid closed, any nosy parkers were left with unsatisfied curiosities.

Detective Inspector Attwood pulled at his collar, clearly feeling the effects of the heat, and then produced a notebook from his pocket. "Chief Inspector Reed, would you mind going through the events of the day? How was it that you ended up here with this trunk on this beach?"

As Basil relayed the day's timetable, Ginger worked out the complications in her head. It could only be pure luck and serendipity that they'd happened to be near the trunk just as the body released enough decomposition gases to raise the trunk to the surface. The adults on the vessel hadn't even been paying attention and might've missed it if it hadn't been for the young lads with them.

And having two suspects on board—because that was what Quentin Bainbridge and Lord Davenport-Witt now were, suspects, along with the rest of the Bainbridge party. Poor Miss Poppy Kerslake. If she thought her day had gone poorly with the earl not inviting her to sail, it was only about to get a lot worse.

The medical examiner and the ambulance arrived, and the circle of onlookers increased.

"Stand back, everyone," Detective Inspector Attwood instructed. "Police business!"

The medical examiner, a middle-aged man with a thick grey moustache, introduced himself as Dr. Johnstone then took a cursory look into the trunk. "I can't tell you anything you don't already know without doing a post-mortem. After that, I should be able to confirm whether the poor bloke was dead or not at the time he was thrown overboard."

Quentin Bainbridge checked his watch. "I've got to let Adeline know. She'll take it hard, poor thing, and her nerves are a nuisance these days."

Soon after Ginger and Basil had returned to their room at the Brighton Seaside Hotel, a telegram came for Basil from Scotland Yard.

"Is it what I think it is?" Ginger asked.

"If you think it's Morris instructing me to lead the investigation into the death of Mr. Austin Bainbridge, then you're correct. The chief constable of East Sussex has made a formal request for the Yard to get involved."

Ginger had a rocky relationship with Superintendent Morris, who found her to be more of a busybody than a help, despite plenty of evidence proving otherwise. For the most part, the two agreed to stay as far apart from each other as possible. Basil, sadly, didn't have that option.

"I hope Detective Inspector Attwood will be all right with that," Ginger said. It wasn't uncommon for Scotland Yard to get involved in difficult murder cases outside London, but that didn't mean the local police didn't get their knickers in a twist over it.

"I suspect he won't be overjoyed," Basil said, "but hopefully, we can work together."

A knock on the door was followed by the flamboyant entrance of Felicia and Ambrosia.

"Was it him?" Felicia pressed her palms together and touched her fingertips to her lips. "Was it Mr. Austin Bainbridge?"

"I'm afraid so," Ginger said, looking beyond the ladies. "Where are Scout and Boss?"

"They're in our room along with Reggie," Felicia said. "I asked room service to bring them up a piece of cake each."

Ginger was appeased. She didn't want talk of this gruesome case to land on young ears.

"I suppose this means our holiday must come to an end," Ambrosia said. "I, for one, find this heat oppressive."

"I'm afraid we'll have to stay for a few days, Lady Gold," Basil said. "I've been assigned the case."

Ambrosia huffed. "Surely this to-do doesn't involve me?"

"She's right," Ginger said. "Could she and Felicia go back to London? They could accompany Scout."

Felicia said, "No," as Ambrosia said, "Yes." The elder Gold lady scowled at the younger. "Why on earth would you want to stay?"

"We've just got here, Grandmama. I've been looking forward to the sun and fresh air."

As if pleading for help, Felicia's gaze darted to Ginger. The trouble was that Ginger knew exactly why Felicia wanted to stay, and it wasn't for the sun and fresh air, but for a certain gentleman, who might be a murderer.

"Well, I'm not chaperoning the boy on my own," Ambrosia said, referring to Scout. She'd never truly got on board with Ginger's decision to adopt a street child. Even though all evidence of Scout's former, humble existence had nearly gone with time, good nutrition, and an excellent education, Ambrosia couldn't forget the small, dirty boy who'd come to them with a strong cockney accent.

"Lizzie can chaperone Scout, and you'll have Langley to assist you," Ginger said.

Ambrosia scowled at Felicia. "Very well," she said, turning on her heel. "If you think you can manage without your maid."

"Thank you," Felicia said, with a spirited grin.

"Don't thank me yet," Ginger said. "You may find you won't like how the investigation turns out."

"Nonsense." Felicia waved her hand as if she were flicking away a pest. "You can't believe the delectable Lord Davenport-Witt had anything to do with it."

Basil's hazel eyes darkened. "I'm afraid this is a

murder investigation, Felicia, and everyone associated with the victim is under suspicion. Perhaps it would be best if you accompanied your grandmother back to London."

Felicia froze, her rosebud lips parting as her heavily made-up eyes stared in disbelief. "I promise to be on my best behaviour, *Chief Inspector.*" Her nose tilted into the air as she addressed Ginger. "I'll be in my room, reading, if you're looking for me. How long do you want me to hold on to your son?"

Oh mercy. Ginger disliked being caught between her by-the-book husband and fly-as-I-fancy sister-in-law.

"We are very grateful to you for helping with Scout on occasion," Ginger said kindly. "I'll fetch him in a few minutes."

When Felicia had left, Ginger turned to Basil. "I'm afraid she has quite a large chip on her shoulder."

"I regret offending her," Basil said. "That wasn't my intent; however, what is to proceed isn't a game, and Felicia must know that."

"She does, love," Ginger said. "She's been so good about avoiding the jazz clubs and night-life lately; you can't blame her for seeking a little diversion."

"I suppose Ambrosia would approve of the earl as Felicia's next suitor," Basil muttered.

"There's little to hold against him," Ginger said.

"He's a gentleman, with money—I presume—and a title . . ." Unfairly, something about Lord Davenport-Witt troubled Ginger, though she couldn't say what for sure. She added reluctantly, ". . . If he's not a murderer, that is."

10

*A*t Basil's request, Attwood notified the friends and family of Austin Bainbridge of their civic duty to stay in Brighton until notified otherwise by officials, and to gather in the meeting room for initial questioning.

A sombre-looking crew sat in a semicircle. Miss Poppy Kerslake sat between Findley and Davenport-Witt, her chair skewed slightly towards the latter, with Bainbridge and his wife to the earl's right. Little Reggie Bainbridge was with Scout and under the watchful eyes of Ambrosia and Felicia. Basil, along with Ginger, claimed two empty chairs while Attwood and his constable stood nearby.

"Thank you for your prompt compliance," Basil said. "For those who don't know, I'm Chief Inspector Reed of Scotland Yard. The local police chief, along with my superintendent, felt it prudent that the Yard gets involved in this investigation and, in that regard, I will be working closely with Detective Inspector Attwood, who has been investigating the disappearance of Mr. Austin Bainbridge. My wife, Mrs. Reed, you probably don't know, is a regular consultant for Scotland Yard. Before we go any further, I must express, on behalf of us all, our deepest condolences on the death of a dear family member and friend."

Mrs. Bainbridge produced the lace handkerchief she'd been gripping and wiped her watery eyes. "I thought there was a chance he might still be alive, perhaps having injured his head somehow and developing amnesia."

Bainbridge tapped her lightly on the knee. "There, there. This will all be over soon." Then to Basil, he said, "Can we please get on with it. You can see how upsetting this is to my wife."

"Of course," Basil said. "This gathering is just to let you all know, officially, that you must remain in Brighton until I say you may leave." He paused long enough that each person felt compelled to nod or shrug, indicating that they understood the instruction. "I will be interviewing each of you alone, so from here, you may go to your rooms and await my arrival. Detective Inspector Attwood and Constable Clarke shall stand by, should you have any further questions."

And to thwart the suspects' compulsion to leave.

"Is this really necessary?" Davenport-Witt asked. "Surely, we can answer whatever questions you may have in this room and be done with it?"

Miss Kerslake nodded her approval at the earl's suggestion with wide, hopeful eyes.

"I'm afraid so," Basil said. "It's a murder investigation now, and it behoves me to ensure that no stone goes unturned."

Findley simply grunted his disapproval. "Might I suggest you start with me? I'd really like to be on my way." He stood, rubbed the creases out of his trousers, and glanced at Basil for consent. "I'll wait in my room."

"I'll be there in ten minutes," Basil said. He'd got a list of the room numbers from Floyd, the manager.

The rest of the room rose to their feet. Davenport-Witt said, "I'll wait for my turn in the hotel lounge, if that's all right with you, Chief Inspector?"

Basil nodded. He figured that by that time, he'd need a drink, himself.

SINCE THE LIFT wasn't large enough to house them all, Basil and Ginger let the Bainbridges, along with Findley and Miss Kerslake, take it first, then many minutes later, followed.

Findley hadn't even bothered to close his door. Out

of courtesy, Basil knocked then stepped in behind Ginger as they entered a large room with a single, neatly made bed, matching wooden furniture and a small seating area, which included a table and four chairs by the window.

"Forgive me," Findley said. "Should I offer drinks? I have a bottle of Scotch to hand."

"That's quite all right," Basil said. He didn't drink whilst on duty, and, at the moment, Ginger had a delicate digestion. "Let us get right to the heart of the matter."

Basil removed a notepad and pencil from his suit pocket and started, "How did you know the deceased?"

Findley slapped at his suit pocket. "Do you mind if I smoke?"

Basil cast a glance at Ginger, who he knew wasn't a fan of cigarette or cigar smoke, but she subtly nodded her head.

"Go ahead," Basil said, wondering why the man was so jittery. Nervousness in a suspect didn't always equate to guilt—some people were just skittish by nature and particularly around authority figures—but sometimes it did.

Findley fussed with his cigarette case, withdrew a handmade cigarette, then fiddled with a lighter, his hand trembling. He inhaled deeply and let out a stream of grey smoke from the side of his mouth. After a moment, where the nicotine seemed to miraculously do its work to bring a sense of calm, Findley answered. "We were business partners."

Basil made a quick notation in his notepad. "What kind of business?"

"Precious gems."

"Selling or investing," Basil asked.

"Both."

"Did you operate from London?" Ginger asked.

"Yes, and here in Brighton. It was why I was included in this farce of a holiday."

"How is business?" Basil asked.

A shrug was followed by another pull on his cigarette. "It's up and down."

"And at the time of Mr. Bainbridge's disappearance," Basil started, "was it up or down?"

Findley snorted, "Down. Now don't take this the wrong way, but Austin didn't exactly have a head for business. The deal? He provided the capital, and I managed things."

"But he didn't keep to his end of the deal?" Ginger said.

"The blighter, er . . ." Mr. Findley cast an uncomfortable glance Ginger's way. Basil was used to people judging him for bringing his wife along to interviews, but he'd learned long ago that a woman's presence often made the interviewee more forthcoming. "Forgive me, madam," Findley said, correcting himself. "Mr. Bainbridge couldn't stop meddling. He was the reason the company lost profits."

"Did he understand this?" Basil asked.

"Yes. However, he had bags of cash and simply didn't care. I, on the other hand . . ."

Ginger offered, "Didn't have bags of cash?"

"No. I didn't. And I don't apologise for it. Some of us have to work for what we have and work hard."

"What happens to the business now, Mr. Findley?" Basil asked.

Mr. Findley groaned. "With the death confirmed, Austin's half of the business will go to his heir, which means I'll have to deal with another meddler."

"Who's his heir?"

"I wouldn't know. His brother, most likely." Findley stabbed an ashtray with the short stub of what remained of his cigarette. "Look here. I know it looks bad . . . like I wanted to get rid of a problem business partner..."

"It's motive," Basil stated.

"Well, yes, but I didn't kill him. I'd rather go bankrupt. I simply don't have the stomach for it."

"Be that as it may," Basil said. "Please don't leave town."

11

*L*eaving a disgruntled Mr. Findley behind with only his cigarettes and bottle of Scotch to keep him company, Ginger and Basil moved on to the Bainbridges' door. Quentin Bainbridge answered Basil's knock.

With a low voice, he whispered, "My wife is sleeping."

Peering around Mr. Bainbridge, Ginger could see a suite like the one she shared with Basil and Scout—their floor plan, though the same, had an opposite layout. A seating area was separated from two sleeping rooms by interior doors.

"We could talk to you," she said, "until your wife wakes up. We'll speak quietly."

Quentin Bainbridge pursed his lips. His apparent dismay at having to accommodate the interview when perhaps he'd hoped for a delay flashed behind his squinty eyes. "Very well." He motioned for Ginger and Basil to enter.

"I had tea brought up," he said. "Would you like a cup?"

"That would be delightful," Ginger said. Mr. Bainbridge stood in for his wife and poured.

After adding milk and sugar, Ginger savoured a sip then said, "Once again, I'd like to offer my sympathies. Finding out about your brother's demise in this fashion must be simply dreadful."

Mr. Bainbridge paled at the memory, and Ginger recalled how he'd been sick at the discovery.

"It's all very ghastly," Quentin Bainbridge said. "But at least now we know."

"How he died?" Basil prompted.

"Well, not that, precisely, only that he did, in fact, die."

"Was there any other logical conclusion?" Basil asked. "Was it like your brother to simply walk away without a word to anyone?"

"My brother was unpredictable at the best of times. I hate to speak ill of him now, but I might as well tell you what you're soon to discover about Austin's character. He was a selfish, inconsiderate blighter without a single ounce of empathy for anyone's suffering, particularly suffering he brought about."

Ginger shifted and crossed her legs at the ankles. "Would you say your brother had any enemies?"

Mr. Bainbridge hedged. "It's not impossible, though I couldn't name any one person specifically. Austin was rather pretentious." His frown deepened. "Not unlike his best pal, Lord Davenport-Witt. Austin often rubbed people the wrong way. But everyone does on occasion, don't they? You don't get killed for it."

"When was the last time you saw your brother alive?" Ginger asked.

There was a pause, then a sip of tea before the man answered. "The morning he disappeared. Austin regularly went for a morning swim, he loved the sea, and that was his big complaint about London. I was picking up our breakfast and morning paper from the corridor when I saw him step into the lift. He didn't see me."

"Was he dressed for swimming?" Ginger asked.

Mr. Bainbridge blinked. "Well, I imagine. I can't really remember."

"So, you just assumed your brother was headed for a morning swim," Basil said. "But you can't verify it."

The poor man looked as if he were about to be sick into his teacup. "I'm afraid not."

Before Ginger or Basil could pursue their line of questioning further, the door flew open, and Reggie ran in. "Daddy. I'm tired of playing with that boy, and I want to go home."

Mr. Bainbridge whipped a finger to his lips. "Shh! Your mother's sleeping."

"She's always sleeping," the boy whined.

Felicia stumbled into the suite with a look of apology. "I'm sorry I couldn't restrain him."

"He tends to get irritable in the afternoon," Mr. Bainbridge said. "He's overstimulated."

Ginger glanced at Basil, witnessing her husband's frustrated facial expression. "Perhaps we'll come back later," she suggested. "When Mrs. Bainbridge is awake, and Reggie is settled."

"That would be best," Mr. Bainbridge said, practically shepherding them towards the door.

Ginger couldn't imagine Adeline Bainbridge sleeping through this commotion, but something told her that Adeline didn't want to talk to the police, and her husband didn't want her to either.

In the corridor, Felicia stared at Ginger and said, "One moment Scout and Reggie are playing cards together like they're lifelong pals, and the next thing I know, Reggie's throwing the cards about, stamping his feet, and insisting on being returned to his parents. I knew you were interviewing, but he ran out before I could stop him."

"It's fine," Ginger said. "We can speak to the Bainbridges again later."

Basil checked his watch and faced Ginger. "We should see to Miss Kerslake, love."

Ginger felt rather fatigued, but she knew that Basil preferred that she accompanied him when he had to speak to ladies like Poppy Kerslake. Not because he didn't trust himself, but because he didn't trust the female in question. Ginger's husband was very attractive, and unscrupulous women were known to throw themselves at him, even when aware that he was a married man.

Sending Basil alone was like sending a lamb to the lions, and Ginger wasn't about to allow that to happen.

Ginger tapped on Miss Kerslake's door while Felicia headed slowly towards her suite. As predicted, the light went out of the starlet's eyes when she saw that Ginger was with Basil. Ginger glanced behind her as she stepped into Miss Kerslake's room, just in time to see Felicia step into the lift.

Oh mercy! Felicia is going to the lounge to meet up with Lord Davenport-Witt!

Ginger could hardly do anything about it now but keep it to herself. Basil wouldn't be very happy with Felicia's interference.

Miss Kerslake wore a delicate sleeveless chiffon frock in a violet hue that accentuated the creamy skin of her slender arms, which were decorated with silver bracelets. A long string of pearls wrapped seductively around her neck and hung long over her flattened bosom.

"Please come in, Chief Inspector." Her full, bright-red lips turned upwards when she added, "Mrs. Reed."

"Thank you, Miss Kerslake," Basil said, his hat in his hands. "We'll be as quick as possible."

Poppy Kerslake strolled elegantly to a chair by the window—her room, similar to Mr. Findley's, was decorated in soft greens and warm yellows.

"Don't hurry on my account," she said after sitting. Then letting her gaze bore into Basil, added, "And you simply must call me Poppy!"

The starlet's insistence on familiarity bordered on vulgar, but Basil, as Ginger expected, answered politely, "Very well, Poppy."

Ginger felt a certain smug satisfaction that Poppy's peacocking didn't have the effect on Basil that Poppy would have hoped for. That didn't stop the starlet from crossing a bare leg—*no stockings*! And dangling a loose, black silk shoe trimmed with rhinestones from her toe. She held Basil's gaze. "I'd offer you something to drink, but alas, my cupboards are bare."

It was an attempt at flirtatious banter as the room lacked a kitchen and thus cupboards, and Poppy was the type to be served not to be of service.

"We've just had tea with Mr. Bainbridge," Ginger said. "Please tell us about the trunk that went missing."

The expression of self-importance dropped from Poppy's face at Ginger's question. There was no point beating about the bush with this one.

Poppy responded coldly. "What do you want to know? The porter took my trunk for storage, and it vanished." She snapped her fingers for dramatic effect, and Ginger couldn't help but notice, once again, how the opal ring sparkled like fire.

"Did any of your other pieces of luggage go missing?" Basil asked.

"No. Just the largest one, which was a pity, since I used it for my shoes and hats that came without boxes."

"Were there any identifying features on the trunk?" Ginger asked.

"What is this about anyway?" Poppy directed her question to Basil. "Why is she going on about my trunk?"

It hadn't yet been disclosed how Austin Bainbridge's body was discovered, so it was a valid question, if rather rudely posed.

"Just answer the question, please," Basil said.

"Fine. It was a Louis Vuitton, branded with the flag of my home country."

Poppy's description confirmed Lord Davenport-

Witt's assertion that the trunk involved in the crime indeed belonged to her.

"How well did you know Austin Bainbridge?"

Poppy smirked. "You could say we had an understanding."

"An understanding?" Ginger asked.

"Yes, I'm sure you know what I mean. We were to be engaged. I do believe that was why he invited me here. Such a romantic place to propose."

"Did Austin Bainbridge give you that ring?" Ginger asked.

Poppy Kerslake held out her hand, stretched out her fingers, and openly admired the jewel. "No. I brought this back from Australia. It's lovely, isn't it?"

"It is," Ginger admitted

"To confirm," Basil started as he glanced down at his notepad, "you were holidaying here in Brighton with the Bainbridge family at Austin Bainbridge's request?"

"Yes."

"What's your relationship with Lord Davenport-Witt?" Ginger asked.

Poppy recrossed her legs with an air of defiance. "What does that have to do with anything?"

"The earl is part of the Bainbridge party, and was also when Austin went missing," Ginger said. "It's relevant."

She raised a brow. "We're *chums*. We met in London."

"Did you meet Mr. Findley before this gathering?" Ginger asked.

"I did."

Ginger cocked her head. "Would you consider him a *chum*?"

Poppy scoffed. "Hardly. Austin said he invited him because they had to attend to business affairs. Mr. Findley isn't exactly one of us."

"Can you think of any reason someone would've wanted Mr. Bainbridge dead?" Basil asked.

"None at all. Austin was, if not loved by all, certainly liked. He had a charming and amiable personality."

Ginger mused at how Miss Kerslake's assessment of Austin Bainbridge was quite the opposite of Quentin Bainbridge's, the deceased's brother. "Why would you say he wasn't loved by all?" she asked.

"Austin could be difficult at times. He drank a bit too much, gambled a bit too much, looked down his nose at those he felt were beneath him. But you could say that about a lot of men. It's not a reason to kill a fella. Though—"

Basil raised a brow. "Though?"

"I did overhear him and Mr. Findley arguing. Austin was shouting obscenities. They'd both been drinking. I'd only gone to the ladies for a few minutes, and when they saw I'd returned, they both suddenly shut like a vault."

Ginger glanced at Basil. Another conversation with Mr. Findley would be in order.

Basil got to his feet, and Ginger followed. "Thank you for your time, er, Poppy," Basil said. "Please don't leave Brighton. I may need to speak to you again."

Poppy smiled seductively. "Anytime, Chief Inspector."

Once they were in the corridor, Ginger let out a huff of disgust. "What a hussy."

"Ginger, love," Basil said, his chin ducked as he looked down at her, his hazel eyes twinkling. "Jealousy is rather unbecoming."

"I know, but she flirted openly with you whilst I, your wife, was sitting right there! Such audacity."

Basil put his arm around Ginger's shoulder and squeezed. "You know there's no one who could ever claim my heart but you."

Ginger sighed as she melted into Basil's side. *I'm emotional again. Since conceiving, I just am not myself.* "And you have mine," she said. "Now, let's check on Scout before he thinks we've abandoned him to Ambrosia!"

12

*J*ust as Ginger had feared, Felicia wasn't in her suite when she and Basil checked up on Scout. Ambrosia had nodded off in a most unsophisticated way—her soft chins high in the air and her thin, wrinkled lips parted.

Scout chortled when he saw Ginger approach and pointed. Ginger put a finger to her mouth, then loudly cleared her throat. Ambrosia's feathers were ruffled, and Ginger purposely focused on Scout and Boss, as if she hadn't just come upon the Dowager Lady Gold mid-snore.

"Hello, Boss," she said as the dog rushed to her side. She scooped him into her arms and rubbed him behind the ears. If it weren't for Boss' affection for Scout, she'd feel guilty leaving him behind so much.

"Can we go to the beach again?" Scout said, hopefully.

"I'm afraid our holiday needs to be cut short," Basil said. "There's been an accident—"

"I know, Aunt Felicia told me all about it. Can't I go swimming once more before we leave for London? Please?"

Ginger knew Basil had to focus on the case, and even if she were up to spending time in the sun, the case before her was too intriguing to ignore.

"Dad and I have to work, but I bet Felicia and Lizzie could go with you and Boss," Ginger said, lowering Boss to the floor. "Would that be all right?"

Scout shrugged. As if it were the best idea in the world, Boss stared back at him with his tongue hanging out. "All right with us."

"But then, you must go back to London tomorrow morning with Lady Gold and Lizzie. No ifs, ands, or buts. Dad and I will join you as soon as we can."

"Where is Felicia?" Ambrosia said. "And I wouldn't mind some tea."

"I'm not sure," Ginger said. "I'll ring the bell for Langley and Lizzie."

Basil excused himself, saying he needed to make a call to Scotland Yard. "I'll meet you in the lounge," he said to Ginger as he left.

Ginger agreed, hoping he didn't get ahead of her

and stumble upon Felicia, who was, no doubt, enjoying the company of one of their suspects.

Langley and Lizzie shortly reported for duty. Ambrosia commissioned Langley to fetch a tea tray, while Ginger took Lizzie to the side and quietly asked her to give Felicia a message. "I believe she may be found in the lounge. Please let her know that I would like to speak to her as soon as possible. I'll be in my suite. Then please prepare to escort Scout to the beach. Be sure he doesn't go in too far."

"Yes, madam." Lizzie curtsied, then rushed off.

As good fortune would have it, the head housekeeper was in the corridor when Ginger, with Scout at her side, stepped into it. As if she intended to pretend she hadn't seen Ginger, the woman quickly turned. *How odd.*

Ginger called out, "Mrs. Merrick?"

Mrs. Merrick stopped and faced Ginger. She had a stack of folded towels in her hands.

"Hello, Mrs. Reed. Are you in need of a fresh towel? Something else?"

The housekeeper wasn't the smiling type, and as her gaze dropped to Scout, her eyes darkened, a look of suppressed pain flashing behind them.

"We have quite enough towels thank you, Mrs. Merrick," Ginger said. "But I hope you have a moment to spare for a quick question."

"Of course," Mrs. Merrick said. "I'm here to make your stay as pleasant as possible."

"Yes, well, my question is about Miss Kerslake's trunk, the one that went missing."

Mrs. Merrick's dark gaze narrowed. "A dreadful affair, that. Someone actually sneaked into the luggage room and stole the trunk. We started locking it after that, I can assure you."

"You've no idea who might've taken it?" Ginger asked.

With a steely look, Mrs. Merrick answered, "None at all. Now, if there's nothing else?"

"That's everything, Mrs. Merrick. Thank you."

As Ginger sauntered back to her suite with Scout at her side, a wave of fatigue overtook her. "Go and get your bathing costume on," she instructed.

As Scout ran off, Ginger took time to wash. A little cold water on the face and a fresh frock would do wonders to re-energise her. She missed having Lizzie to assist her—doing the buttons at the back was tricky—but fortunately, Ginger was the flexible sort and managed to relieve herself of her outfit. She chose a casual Jean Lanvin frock with simple lines dropping at the waist.

With fresh lipstick and new rouge on her cheeks, Ginger felt she looked as good as new. She'd just entered the sitting area of the suite when Felicia tapped on the door and let herself in.

"You require my presence?" Felicia asked with the tone of one who's been insulted.

"I do," Ginger said. "Were you busy with something? Or should I say, some*one*?"

Felicia's gaze darted to the side. "I don't know what you mean."

"Can you honestly tell me you didn't go to the lounge to seek out Lord Davenport-Witt?"

"So, what if I did? It's not like a bit of friendly conversation is going to alter your investigation. And did it occur to you that perhaps I might find out a bit of information that may be of interest to you? Surely, the earl would be more forthcoming with me than being interrogated by the two of you."

Ginger thought Felicia might have a point. "And did you?"

Felicia pouted. "Well, it's not like I want him to be guilty of anything. He did tell me that he and Poppy Kerslake were only friends, which I have to say delighted me to bits, and that he and Austin Bainbridge were good friends from university."

Ginger worked her lips. Not exactly significant news, though she suspected Poppy Kerslake wanted to change that relationship status. A man with a title and means wasn't wanting for female attention. Perhaps the earl was a man of some scruples who wouldn't betray his good friend by taking up with his girl, but if the fellow were out of the way? Could Poppy have believed the earl would come to her if Austin weren't around? Did she see herself and Lord Davenport-Witt as future lovers pushed together by tragic circumstances?

Which made Ginger wonder why the earl had remained unmarried? He was at least Ginger's age and eligible.

"All of that's neither here nor there at the moment," Ginger responded. "I hope you'll be willing to accompany Scout and Lizzie to the beach for an hour or so. I promised he could go one more time before leaving, and Basil and I simply can't."

"It's not like I have anything else to do." Felicia smiled crookedly in the way she did when she was about to tease. "And there's always a nice show of handsome men frolicking about."

13

*D*avenport-Witt could be a patient man when he wanted to, at least that was Basil's assessment when he and Ginger finally met up with the earl, who by now was sipping an amber beverage. Basil couldn't be certain just what number the drink constituted, but by the glossy shimmer in the man's eyes, he'd wager a guess it wasn't his first.

"Ah, the Reed family arrives at last," Davenport-Witt said with a nod of his head. He raised his glass. "Can I order you a drink, old chap? Madam?"

"Perhaps, when we've finished with our questions," Basil said. He enjoyed a brandy or other spirits at the end of the workday, but one had to keep one's mind clear whilst on the job.

"As you wish." Davenport-Witt sipped gingerly

then smiled with pleasure as he swallowed. "Ah. Hits the spot, doesn't it?"

Basil and Ginger joined Davenport-Witt, each claiming a leather-backed chair. A chessboard sat on the table, clearly abandoned mid-game, though a cursory glance confirmed to Basil that the black team, apparently the earl's colour, would've won in less than five moves.

The room was windowless, and the lighting dim, yet the glimmering crystal lamps provided an inviting ambience. A female jazz singer cooed in the background.

"I understand that you and our victim, Austin Bainbridge, were long-time friends," Basil said.

"That's true," Davenport-Witt admitted, "and oh, how it pinches to hear him referred to as a victim. He would've hated that."

"Oh?" Ginger prompted.

"Austin wasn't the type of bloke to be found at the bottom of the pile if you know what I mean. He was always at the top. Wouldn't settle for less."

"It's rather lonely at the top, isn't it?" Ginger asked.

"Indeed, if it's a pinnacle," Davenport-Witt said with a grin. "And with Austin, it always was."

"I imagine he wasn't alone in wanting that spot," Basil said. "A rather competitive position?"

Davenport-Witt smirked. "What, kind sir, are you suggesting?"

"If more than one man wants to be king, a battle must ensue," Basil said.

"You're suggesting that someone knocked Austin off his pinnacle?" Davenport-Witt snorted. "I can assure you that it wasn't me. I'd rather play with the peasants." The earl chuckled. "Theoretically, I've got no interest in power for power's sake. Though, if you consider the competition amongst brothers—"

"Are you saying that Austin was at odds with Quentin?" Ginger asked.

Lord Davenport-Witt lifted a shoulder. "Quentin's a bit of a wet fish, but he is the younger of the two. I know it's surprising, isn't it? Unlike Austin, he inherited his father's receding hairline. That, and with a wife and child, everyone just assumed he was the eldest brother. And now he's the heir to the Bainbridge fortune."

Basil caught Ginger's eye. It was a good motive.

"Poppy Kerslake led us to believe that she and Austin had an understanding," Ginger said. "She thought he'd invited her to Brighton to propose."

The earl laughed heartily. "That's news to me. The Austin Bainbridge I knew refused to be tied to just one woman. I'm afraid Miss Kerslake would've been kept waiting a long time."

Basil stilled. If Poppy Kerslake had learned that Austin wasn't going to make her his wife, could she have become angry enough to kill him? Basil pivoted to a new subject, a sometimes-effective technique to upset an interviewee's equilibrium, and asked, "How well do you know Mr. Findley?"

"That stuffy old shirt? Not well. I met him on occasion in London whilst in the company of Austin."

"You didn't approve of Austin Bainbridge's association with Mr. Findley?" Ginger asked.

"Ah, that was just another lost cause for Austin. He was in the habit of getting into soft business ventures that were doomed to fail. It was a major bone of contention between the brothers. Quentin accused him of reckless disregard for the family coffers."

"Can you think of anyone who would want to see Austin dead?" Basil asked. "Besides his brother or business partner."

Davenport-Witt downed the rest of his drink. "I can't say that I can. Austin was a lover, not a fighter. He could be a bit short-sighted when it came to the feelings of other earthly sojourners, but who isn't from time to time? Now, is there anything else?"

Basil shook his head. "That will be all for now, Lord Davenport-Witt, but please don't leave Brighton."

"Understood. Good day, then, Chief Inspector Reed, Mrs. Reed."

As the earl stepped away, Ginger called after him. "Lord Davenport-Witt?"

"Yes?"

"Have we met before? I feel like I should know you, but I can't think from where?"

Something flashed behind the earl's eyes, and a twitch in his cheek hinted at a note of danger.

"Sadly, I don't believe I've had the pleasure," he said. "I have a familiar face and, on occasion, have been reported on in the society pages." The devil-may-care expression returned. "Believe me, madam, if we'd met, I would've remembered you."

After the man had left, Basil stared down at his wife. "What is it, love?"

"I find him unsettling, and it troubles me that I can't put a finger on why."

Leaving the lounge, Ginger and Basil strolled through the reception area towards the lift. The manager rested his pen on the desk when he saw them, his face breaking into a friendly smile. "Good afternoon, Chief Inspector and Mrs. Reed. I hope everything is to your liking here at the Brighton Seaside Hotel. Is there anything I can do for you?"

Ginger tugged on Basil's arm and whispered. "We've yet to question Mr. Floyd."

Basil mumbled back. "Now is as good a time as any." Then loudly, "Good afternoon, Mr. Floyd. We are well, thank you."

Ginger and Basil approached the desk, and Ginger ensured they were set apart from other guests meandering by. "Would you mind if we asked you a few questions?" she said. "It'll only take a moment."

The manager blinked, his thin moustache stretching over a mouth that tightened subtly before relaxing into his familiar grin. "Of course. Anything I can do to help, I will."

"You're aware, of course," Basil began, "that I'm now here on official police business."

"Yes, the kind inspector did inform me of the dreadful turn of events. The management has expressed our deepest sympathies to the family."

"How long have you worked here?" Ginger asked.

"Since 1919." Mr. Floyd laughed carefully. "I've seen a great number of changes since then."

Ginger smiled back. "As we all have, I'm sure. How often does the Bainbridge family come to Brighton on holiday? Annually? Or was this the first time?"

"Hmm, I wouldn't say annually, though they may have, regrettably, stayed at a competitor's hotel. But a few times over the last few years, certainly."

"What did you think of Mr. Austin Bainbridge?" Basil asked.

The manager's head jerked back. "Oh, it's not my business to make judgements on our guests. I couldn't say I thought anything about him at all."

Basil leaned casually against the counter. "You're not a machine, Mr. Floyd, and, I would say, you're quite adept at making sound character judgements. You must have had a few thoughts regarding the deceased."

The poor manager swallowed hard, his Adam's apple bouncing in response. His face reddened at Basil's request, and Ginger felt a twinge of pity.

"I can't really say," Mr. Floyd finally said, "besides, it's uncouth to speak ill of the dead."

Ginger gazed back with sympathy. "Mr. Floyd, the chief inspector and I both understand that a man in your position must value a guest's privacy and keep all secrets as a matter of principle. However, this is a murder enquiry. The fact that you don't want to speak ill of the dead suggests that there was, in fact, something ill of which to speak."

Mr. Floyd let out a defeated breath. "Very well, Mr. Austin Bainbridge would ask me to cover for him, on occasion."

"Cover?" Basil said. "As in lie?"

"Yes. He didn't want his brother to know that he visited . . . er . . ." He lowered his voice. ". . . Gambling rooms. If Mr. Quentin Bainbridge should ask if I'd seen him, I was to say he'd gone swimming."

"The morning of his disappearance," Ginger started, "did Mr. Austin Bainbridge go swimming?"

"I would say not. He most certainly wasn't dressed for the beach, at any rate."

"Did he say where he was going?"

"No, madam. I wish he had. I would've told him the tide was too high for swimming. It was a blustery day. Dangerous for both swimming and sailing."

14

"I'm sure we could make it to the train station without being chaperoned by you."

As the Gold family's matriarch and head of the house for so many years, Ambrosia had developed a strong-headed tenacity as a means of survival. When the Gold family fortunes turned because of the unbeknown gambling habits of both her husband and son, Ambrosia had found a way to conceal their hardships and save their reputation. When Lord Gold died, she was left to manage the estate and keep it from the brink of bankruptcy. When her son and daughter-in-law suffered their tragic carriage accident, it was Ambrosia who, though ageing, had taken on the role of mother to Felicia and Daniel.

And Ambrosia had commissioned Daniel to marry for money to save Bray Manor, their family estate, which was how Ginger and Daniel had met. To look at the Dowager Lady Gold, with pursed lips, and soft chin jutting upwards, one would be forgiven if one were to surmise that the lady had lived a life of ease and luxury, but they'd be wrong.

Ginger couldn't forget that her grandmother-in-law was no longer a youth. She was a little remorseful about taxing the elderly Gold lady with the role of the leader in this entourage, which included young Scout and the two maids—Lizzie and Langley—and Boss, who was following Scout's heels.

"No one is arguing about your capability, Grand-mother," Ginger said gently. "And we're coming to see Scout off, not you, if that makes you feel any better."

Basil had said his goodbyes, needing to hurry off to a meeting at the police station.

Ambrosia harrumphed; the soft jowls around her pursed lips moved gently. "I still don't understand why Felicia isn't returning as well. Langley and Lizzie will be in third class. Am I to chaperone a boy and a dog on my own?"

Ginger felt her chest tighten. Even though she and Basil had legally adopted Scout, Ambrosia failed to embrace him as one of theirs. She couldn't shake the knowledge that Scout had come to them as a charity case, a street orphan who initially worked with the staff at Hartigan House and had slept in the attic.

"It's a short trip," Ginger said. "And Boss is staying with me."

"Ah, Mum," Scout interjected.

Ginger knelt and spoke softly. "Grandmother is right. She needn't look after a boy and a dog."

"But I'll take care of Boss."

Boss, hearing his name, knew he was the topic of conversation. He tilted his head, his short tail wagging like a furry thumb keeping one-quarter time. Ginger patted his head.

"I know, and you'd do a terrific job. However, Boss is needed here, to help Dad and me solve the case. You know how good he is at sniffing out clues."

This made the young lad smile. "You won't stay behind for long, I hope?" he asked.

"With Boss' help, I'm sure we'll have finished here in no time."

"I wish I didn't have to go. I like the seaside."

Ginger kissed her son's wheat-coloured head. "We'll come again. I promise. Besides," Ginger pointed to the sky. A bruised bank of clouds was rolling in on the horizon. "The weather's changing. You'd have to stay inside the hotel room the whole time, and that wouldn't be fun. Plus, I need you to check on Goldmine for me."

Goldmine was Ginger's Akhal-Teke, a rare and extraordinarily beautiful horse breed. Goldmine was the colour of sunshine with a thick golden mane, and Scout had grown very fond of the stallion. Summoning the horse's name was the right thing to do as Scout's disposition immediately changed.

"Can I ride him, Mum?"

"Only with Clement watching."

Clement was the gardener and occasional chauffeur. Scout happily agreed to the terms.

It took two taxicabs to get the travellers and their luggage to the station, and by the time they were all safely on board the train, Ginger felt fatigued.

"Shall we stop for tea?" Felicia offered.

"That sounds like an excellent idea," Ginger said.

"There's a teashop by that boutique I told you about." Felicia linked her arm with Ginger's. "I can't stop thinking about that frock. You can have a look before I buy it."

THE WIND off the sea was brisk, and Ginger was glad she'd donned her rose and green plaid spring coat. As it was, she held Boss tightly to her chest for extra warmth.

"Perhaps we should head back to the hotel," she said. "I'd hate to get caught in a downpour."

Felicia glanced up at the sky. "I think we have time. We'll skip the tea. We can get that at the hotel later."

Against Ginger's better judgement, she consented. "But only because I'm frightfully curious about this frock. You've got my expectations up."

Felicia grinned. "You won't be disappointed!"

It was a short taxicab ride to the boutique, which was walking distance from the hotel. Ginger paid the man before stepping onto the pavement. "I hope the shop owner doesn't mind that I have Boss with me."

Felicia frowned. "Keep him under your coat. You'll look rather a lot farther along than you are, but no one will question you."

Ginger shot her a look. "Until my belly barks."

"Boss? Surely not."

Ginger couldn't keep her sense of pride over her pet from tickling her lips. Boss was tremendously intelligent and well trained. She placed a finger to her lips, her sign for Boss to stay silent, before tucking him under her coat lapels and out of sight.

The dress shop catered to seaside-goers with a variety of summer frocks, sun hats, and accessories. It was quaint in size and décor and rather crowded with shoppers and supplies.

Ginger couldn't help but compare it to Feathers & Flair, her own two-floor Regent Street shop in London, which had marble floors, large electric chandeliers, and gold-embossed trim. This store was a single-floor facsimile of many others Ginger had visited; however, it lacked a certain finesse found in city shops, being what one could call quaint.

However, the frock was fantastic. The satin crepe georgette dress was deep jade green with sheer sleeves and a matching low-waist belt tied in a pretty bow on the left hip. The cuffs and square low-cut neckline were adorned with contrasting beads of rose and pearl, and a tasteful amount of beading was found on the bow. The only serious problem was it was no longer displayed on a mannequin but on the live body of Miss Poppy Kerslake!

"Miss Gold, Mrs. Reed," the starlet said coolly.

Felicia's eyes narrowed in vexation. "I thought you weren't supposed to leave the hotel, Miss Kerslake."

Poppy Kerslake snorted. "I was told not to leave Brighton. One must continue living and shopping as it were." She twirled for effect. "What do you think? Isn't it simply fabulous?"

"I've seen nicer frocks," Felicia returned. "You must visit Ginger's shop, Feathers & Flair, when you're back in London. Nothing here quite compares."

Felicia's recommendation delighted Ginger, but she could've done without Poppy Kerslake's contempt.

"I've been there." Poppy flicked a hand as if to brush the memories away. "I rather like this little shop."

"It's nice," Ginger said, not wanting to sound spiteful. "But Felicia's right. The colour of that frock isn't very flattering with your overall look. Do you have a stylist? I could recommend someone."

Poppy stared back in horror. "Of course, I have a stylist. And I'm quite certain she'd approve of this frock." Poppy examined her image in the mirror again. "But perhaps you're right. The overall look is rather juvenile, isn't it?"

Poppy disappeared into the changing room, and Felicia let out a raspberry. "I don't know if I even want that frock anymore. It feels tainted."

Poppy returned, the lovely jade green frock hanging over one arm. She handed it to the shop assistant. "I'll take it."

She cast a victorious glance over her shoulder at Felicia. "I saw you admiring it the other day."

Felicia's lips bunched together, holding in whatever vitriol threatened to burst forth, and Ginger had to give her sister-in-law credit for refusing to make a scene. She patted Felicia on the arm and spoke quietly. "Let's not be petty. There are plenty of frocks to go around."

Though, because of the war, the same couldn't be said of men. Ginger shivered at the competitive glares Felicia and Poppy stabbed at each other.

Boss, sensing the negative mood, wiggled under Ginger's coat.

"What's that?" Poppy said.

Boss' head poked out.

"It's my dog," Ginger replied.

"I don't think pets are allowed in the shop."

"You're quite right," Ginger said. "Felicia darling, let's leave Miss Kerslake to complete her purchase. You've promised me a tea."

Before they left, Ginger turned back to Poppy Kerslake. "You grew up in Australia. I hear sailing is all the rage there. Do you know how to sail, Miss Kerslake?"

Miss Kerslake's lips pursed. "Of course."

"How lovely," Ginger responded. As she left Poppy Kerslake behind in the shop, she thought about how the starlet could've acquired a sailing boat and delivered the body of Austin Bainbridge, tucked away in her trunk, into the English Channel.

15

"**M**r. Floyd," Basil said, waving the manager over. "What's the weather forecast for today? It's looking rather bleak outside."

"Big storm rolling in from the south. Such a disappointment for our tourists. Puts a right damper on their plans. I'm afraid guests are checking out early. Is there anything else I can assist you with? Otherwise, the desk is rather busy."

Basil adjusted his trilby hat. "Would you ring for a taxicab?"

"Of course," Floyd said with a bow. "It would be my pleasure."

Basil intended to meet Attwood at the police station to share notes but found that lingering in the lobby as he waited for his taxicab was informative. Unhappy travellers were indeed ending their holidays early. In a vigorous rhythm, Cooper, the porter, moved luggage to waiting vehicles with their boots open in anticipation. Hats were donned, and unseasonable jackets were worn. Ladies pointed, children cried, and men frowned.

For Basil, the removal of persons who proved to clutter his investigation was a fortunate situation. It was best if only his prime suspects were left to wiggle and squirm under the spotlight of open space and poorly attended gatherings.

A fortuitous lull in the departure sequence gave Basil opportunity to call Cooper to his attention.

The porter's eyes flashed with annoyance. Perhaps he intended to use the lull for personal use; however, he quickly recovered and smiled as he politely responded. "Good morning, Chief Inspector Reed—or not so good if the weather's not to your liking."

Basil glanced out of the glass doors spotted with rivulets of rain. "Yes, such a shame," he said.

Cooper's eyebrows jumped with expectancy. "Can I help you with something, sir?"

"How long have you worked at the Brighton Seaside Hotel, Mr. Cooper?"

"Two years, sir, since the summer of twenty-four."

"Have you worked as a porter the whole time?"

"Yes, sir."

"Then you were on duty here when the Bainbridge

party arrived?"

"I was, sir." He tugged on his lapels. "It was the first time I'd ever seen Miss Poppy Kerslake in person. I was a bit rattled at first since just the night before, I'd watched her latest film at the cinema."

"Did Miss Kerslake arrive alone?"

"No, sir. She came with Mr. Austin Bainbridge."

"And the other members of the party?"

"Mr. Quentin Bainbridge, his wife, and son had arrived before them and were already settled in their suite. Lord Davenport-Witt arrived within minutes of Miss Kerslake, and he and Mr. Austin Bainbridge exchanged pleasant greetings. Mr. Findley arrived as the earl was checking in."

"And were pleasant greetings exchanged between the gentlemen as well?" Basil asked.

The porter shook his head. "They didn't show any signs of knowing each other at the time."

"A man in your position likely sees plenty," Basil said with an encouraging smile. Staff in hotels such as this were often overlooked by guests—treated as if they were invisible. He'd learned from Ginger the importance of acknowledging even the lowliest chambermaid with a smile and a friendly hello. "Did you notice anything unusual?"

"Oh," Cooper glanced away. "I can't really say, can I? It's hotel policy to keep our guests' affairs private."

"I understand, but this is a murder investigation. I can assure you that what you share will stay with me unless it's needed as evidence in the court of law. Your employment is secure, Mr. Cooper."

The porter nervously glanced at the desk, and Basil noted that, fleetingly, Floyd frowned in their direction before another group of guests demanded his attention. The stack of luggage meant Cooper's time was short.

"Well, I'm not an expert on love, sir, but it seemed to me that the way Miss Kerslake flirted with Lord Davenport-Witt would've bothered even the most placid man."

Floyd summoned Cooper before he could elaborate, and he hurried to the front desk just as a cabbie stepped into the lobby.

"Taxicab for a Chief Inspector Reed."

Basil acknowledged the cabbie with a nod and followed him outside.

By the time the taxicab pulled up in front of the police station, the rain fell in angry torrents. It'd been difficult to see out of the fogged-up windows in the back seat, and Basil felt a little unnerved that he hadn't been able to make a mental note of the route. They'd circled the roundabout in front of the aquarium with its distinctive clock tower spire, then gone inland, making quick turns here and there. The police station itself was small and nondescript, especially when compared to so many of the town's landmarks.

Inside the small lobby, Basil removed his hat, shook the rain off, and put the trilby back on his head. An officer stared at him with questioning eyes. "Can I help you, sir?"

"Chief Inspector Reed to see Detective Inspector Attwood."

"Ah, you're from Scotland Yard," the officer said, a glimmer of awe passing behind his eyes. "I'll fetch him for you."

Attwood appeared and extended his hand. "Good day, Chief Inspector. I apologise for the shoddy weather."

Basil grinned. "I'm certain the Brighton police can't take responsibility for that."

"You'd be surprised what we get blamed for around here. Coppers get the short end of the stick most of the time."

Basil conceded that that was true, but sadly, if one went by historical example, public distrust wasn't always without merit. Basil meant to change that, as much as possible, though one man could only do so much to turn the tide of public opinion.

"Can I offer you a cup of tea, Chief Inspector?"

Basil removed his hat, gloves, and overcoat. "That

would be most welcome. Milk and sugar, if you don't mind."

The detective inspector stuck his head out of the door, barked at one of the officers, then returned to his desk. He rubbed his chin, already showing shadowing with new beard growth, then asked, "Any breaks on the case?"

Basil lifted a shoulder. "Just fact-finding, at the moment. No one has come out and confessed to murder, I'm afraid."

Attwood chuckled. "That would be too easy now, wouldn't it?"

The teas arrived, and Basil took a sip before continuing. "What do you know about the brother?"

Attwood opened a desk drawer and removed a file. "Financial checks came back. Quentin Bainbridge appears clean as a whistle. No large debts, no defaulted payments. His investments are legitimate and doing well."

"No financial reason to need access to his inheritance then?" Basil asked. It was the only motive he had for Quentin Bainbridge.

The detective inspector cradled his mug, blew on the brew, and then took a tentative sip. "Not from that angle, anyway."

"What do you mean?"

"Austin Bainbridge's financials were a different

story. He certainly had plenty of money to live a lavish and lazy lifestyle, but it turns out he wanted to invest in a diamond mine in South Africa. Sight unseen."

"Quentin probably wasn't too happy about that, I gather," Basil said.

"According to Mrs. Merrick, the head housekeeper, they had quite a row about it." Attwood grinned slyly. "Those alcoves in the corridors make for good hiding places."

"Do you think Quentin would kill his brother to keep him from making a poor investment?" Basil asked.

Attwood shrugged. "Perhaps not intentionally."

"We need a cause of death," Basil said. "Assuming Austin Bainbridge was killed before being inserted into Miss Kerslake's trunk, or at least we must presume he was unconscious. Hard to imagine a conscious man stepping into such a tight spot without a fight." The thought of being trapped in a confined space made Basil chill. "Have you heard from your medical examiner, Dr. Johnstone?"

"I called him this morning. He's working on it. Bloated corpses are a difficult job, I presume. Hopefully, we'll find out more by tomorrow."

"Did you learn anything about Lionel Findley?"

"Middle-class bloke who's out of his league with these folks, I reckon. Series of failed business ventures. This one . . ." Attwood shuffled pages in his file. ". . .

Gems International had potential, but Austin Bainbridge kept messing things up and losing investors. At least, that's what Findley reported when I interviewed him. According to his report, Bainbridge would miss important meetings with clients, and his devil-may-care attitude made the money men lose their trust in their foreign ventures."

"That leaves Miss Kerslake," Basil said.

"Typical gold-digger. Actress from Australia hoping to make it big in films in England. Makes headway as far as fame goes, but her bank balance isn't large enough to support the lifestyle she likes and wants her fans to see."

"She needs access to deep pockets," Basil said.

"Rather needy is what I was told. According to Findley, Austin was growing tired of her."

And she of him, Basil mused. "It always seems to come back to her," he said. "I have a hard time believing she could pull this off on her own."

"Quite," Attwood said. "One of those chaps must have had a hand in it."

"Quentin, Davenport-Witt, or Findley?"

"Exactly," Attwood said.

Basil put his empty mug on Attwood's desk and stood. "You've been terribly helpful, Detective Inspector. Thank you."

"You're welcome. Any time, sir."

16

*H*ow serendipitous that Ginger and Felicia's taxicab would pull up to the front of the hotel at the very same moment Basil had returned. When he saw them, he opened Ginger's door and held up a black umbrella.

"Thank you, love," Ginger said. "Ghastly turn in the weather."

Holding her umbrella over her head, Felicia exited the taxicab and hurried into the hotel without so much as a "how do you do".

Heading to the hotel entrance, Ginger held Boss under one arm and grasped Basil's arm with the other. "Speaking of a ghastly turn in the weather, Felicia's got her bonnet in a blizzard."

"Did something happen at the train station?"

The porter held the door open before Ginger could

answer. "Good afternoon, Chief Inspector, Mrs. Reed."

"Thank you," Ginger said.

Basil collapsed the umbrella and gave it to Mr. Cooper, who placed it into the brass umbrella holder.

The lobby was unusually quiet, and a glance into the lounge as they walked by showed an empty room.

"Where is everyone?" Ginger asked.

"The storm has frightened most of the guests away," Basil said. "Our suspects, of course, must remain, but it may just be us on the second floor tonight."

"How eerie."

"It's just a storm. So why is Felicia up in arms?"

They stepped into the lift, and the attendant, already knowing their floor number, pushed the knob engraved with the number two.

"We had a rather unpleasant encounter with Miss K—" Ginger cast a glance at the attendant who astutely looked straight ahead with a blank expression on his face, "—with a certain lady at a dress shop. The lady and our miss appear to be interested in the same gentleman."

"Oh," Basil said.

Ginger would give him more details once they were in their room. She smiled at the attendant. "Mr.

Weaver, how long have you worked as a lift operator at this hotel?"

"Seven years, madam, since it opened.."

"You were then witness to the affairs that occurred around Mr. Austin Bainbridge's disappearance?"

"I was, indeed, madam."

Ginger looked at Basil, who nodded, willing her to go ahead with her questioning.

"Did you notice anything untoward leading up to the sad event?" she continued. "Anything unusual or out of the ordinary?"

The bell rang, indicating the lift cage had arrived at their floor.

"I make it a point not to notice things, madam."

The grate of the outer door opened, and Basil stretched out a hand as if he were keeping it so. Mr. Weaver shifted, his white-gloved hand poised over the down button.

Ginger smiled. "I'm sure you do, Mr. Weaver, and it's a very commendable quality for one in your position. However, you are only human."

Basil added, "If you can help us with a murder investigation, you must do so."

Mr. Weaver's jaw tightened. "I can't really say. It would be wrong for me to shed an ill light on one of my own."

Ginger blinked. *One of his own?* "Do you mean to say a member of staff acted out of order?"

"I saw Cooper with the trunk you were asking about—the one belonging to the actress. He came out of the stairwell on the ground floor with it hoisted over one shoulder. It was so large and awkward that it covered his face, and he didn't see me coming out of the staff loo."

"Where did he go with it?"

"I don't know. Out the back, I would think. At the time, I presumed he was on an errand for Miss Kerslake. Our guests often ask personal favours from the staff."

Things are looking dire for Miss Kerslake, Ginger thought. "Thank you, Mr. Weaver." Ginger removed a sixpence from her purse and slipped it into the attendant's hand. "You've been most helpful."

Once they entered their suite, a sense of fatigue overwhelmed Ginger. "I miss the days when my energy seemed endless." She flopped into an armchair and pushed off her shoes, one at a time. Boss had the same idea and curled up on her lap.

"I'll ring for tea," Basil said. "It's lunchtime, as well. The chicken is good."

"Sounds delightful."

Ginger relaxed one hand on the armrest, allowing her fingers to dangle over the side. With the other, she patted Boss on the head. He nudged his wet nose under her hand and let out a soft whine.

"I know, Bossy," Ginger said, scrubbing her pet's ears. "I miss Scout too. We shan't be here long, I hope."

As they waited for room service to arrive, Basil brought Ginger a glass of water then settled into a matching chair.

"What do we know, or think we know, so far?" Ginger asked.

"Our first clue is the trunk the body was found in, belonging to Poppy Kerslake."

Ginger agreed. "Lord Davenport-Witt recognised it."

Basil crossed his legs and inclined his head. "Because he put Austin inside and helped Miss Kerslake carry it?"

"She needed someone's help," Ginger said. "But why would Lord Davenport-Witt immediately admit to his knowledge of it? It would be more natural for a guilty person to remain silent."

"Unless he knew an investigation would be initiated and possibly come around to him?"

"A defensive manoeuvre?"

"Davenport-Witt is a chess man. He knows how to think several moves ahead."

Ginger recalled the chess game the earl had apparently been playing in the lounge when they'd first questioned him.

"I admit there's something about the earl that unsettles me," Ginger said. "And it's not because Felicia is smitten. I'd be happy for her to find a proper husband, and normally, an earl with enough intelligence to win at chess would be a fine candidate."

"What is it that bothers you?"

"I can't really say, and that troubles me more. I get the feeling we've met, yet, I can't recall where, and you heard him deny it."

"Perhaps he has a doppelgänger."

Ginger conceded that must be the case, and quite likely, she'd met that doppelgänger in France.

A knock on the door presented a maid with a trolley containing their lunch and tea. Basil tipped the woman, then pushed the trolley towards Ginger. "Don't get up, love," he said.

With adoration flooding her heart, Ginger watched Basil prepare her tea the way she liked it then fill a plate with a portion of chicken and spring salad.

"You're too good to me!" she gushed as she accepted her cup.

"Nothing is too good for my wife and the mother of my child. I worry, Ginger, that you do too much."

"What am I doing? Going to the beach or the shops with Felicia?"

"You know what I mean."

"This case? Asking questions is hardly taxing, darling."

They ate in silence for a bit, and though Ginger had moved Boss to the floor, she sneaked him a piece of chicken, and he licked her fingers in appreciation.

Basil raised a brow but wisely kept his comments to himself. Instead, he said, "Speaking of Felicia; please expand on your adventure with Miss Kerslake."

Ginger snorted then covered her mouth with her fingers. "Erm, it began with them both wanting the same frock and ended with them wanting the same man."

"Davenport-Witt."

"Yes, and Miss Kerslake took a singular delight in robbing Felicia of any hope of either item."

"Poppy Kerslake has motive," Basil said. "According to Attwood, the acting profession doesn't make her the kind of money she needs to live the lifestyle she likes to portray. If Austin Bainbridge was tiring of her, perhaps she changed her sights to Davenport-Witt. Certainly, the porter's observations suggest such a thing."

"But surely, she didn't need to kill him to do that."

"I agree—it's where the theory breaks down. Unless he scorned her in some fashion, and she lashed out in a moment of passion."

"Do we know cause of death?" Ginger asked.

Basil shook his head. "Not yet."

"By the state of the body," Ginger said, "the autopsy is probably a challenge."

"Indeed," Basil replied. "However, let's not get over-focused on Poppy Kerslake. There are other suspects with greater motives and means. Austin's propensity to make poor financial decisions drained the family finances, and according to Attwood, Mrs. Merrick witnessed a serious row between the brothers."

"But why would Quentin suggest that he saw his brother leave for an apparent swim, but not dressed for swimming? It unravels the presumption of accidental death."

"Except that we now know it wasn't accidental."

"True, but it's still the offering up of unnecessary details if one were guilty." Ginger refilled the teacups with tea. "Poppy Kerslake reported that she saw Austin and Mr. Findley arguing."

"Attwood confirmed that Austin wanted to invest in a diamond mine in South Africa, possibly with the funds he'd promised to Findley."

"Did Quentin know about that?" Ginger asked.

"Apparently."

"Motive, again."

"Indeed."

Ginger placed her empty plate on the side table then patted her thigh, calling Boss to jump up once again. "And now we have Mr. Weaver reporting that Mr. Cooper made off with Miss Kerslake's trunk." Boss curled on her lap and closed his eyes. "How on earth is the porter involved?"

"I'm afraid we have a lot of investigating yet to do, Lady Gold." Basil's hazel eyes twinkled at the use of Ginger's professional name.

Ginger started back from under her eyelashes. "The game's afoot."

The storm was a deterrent to dining out so when Ginger, Basil, and Felicia entered the hotel restaurant, they found that all their suspects had made the same decision. Letting out a bout of laughter, Lord Davenport-Witt seemingly enjoyed the company of Miss Kerslake and Mr. Findley as the three sat together at a nearby table.

Clearly not sharing the humour, Mr. Findley's lips pulled into a tense half-grin, but Miss Kerslake was all smiles and giggles. Her elegant black evening dress had a wide band of sequins on the scooped neckline which sparkled in the candlelight. Felicia squirmed and whispered in Ginger's ear. "See, she's not even wearing the frock she bought to spite me."

The Bainbridge family, all three with dour expressions on their faces, occupied a table on the other side of the room, which was uncharacteristically empty for this time of year.

Ginger made sure to smile politely and nod at patrons as Basil chose a table for them, strategically in the middle where one could watch and possibly listen in on one's neighbours.

The earl and his companion captivated Felicia's focus, and Ginger had to nudge her gently. "Don't stare, darling, it's rude and unbecoming."

Felicia huffed, picked up the menu, and mumbled into its spine. "I don't understand what he sees in her."

"Well," Ginger stared with a note of teasing in her voice, "she is beautiful and charming with a certain amount of talent."

Felicia glared but wisely said nothing in response.

A waiter approached, asking for their drinks order, which they gave. Ginger was inclined to drink soda water, her stomach rejecting all her usual choices of beverage. Brandy and wine made her feel particularly bilious. Her friend Matilda, the wife of her good friend Reverend Oliver Hill, was a former medical student who volunteered on occasion as a midwife. She had reassured Ginger that odd cravings and unusual dislikes in foods usually enjoyed were normal for ladies in Ginger's condition.

Their drinks arrived, and their dinner orders were taken.

"Is it me," Basil said, "or do Mr. and Mrs. Bainbridge appear particularly taken with the other table? And not happily, I'd say."

"I've noticed the same thing," Ginger said. "There's no love lost between Adeline Bainbridge and Poppy Kerslake. If you recall my mentioning after we arrived, Felicia and I spotted Adeline fleeing the hotel in tears when Poppy descended the stairs."

Felicia supported Ginger's statement with a tight nod.

The food arrived, and when they had finished eating, Ginger reached over and placed a gloved hand on Basil's arm. "Perhaps we should say a proper hello."

"Divide and conquer?" He tugged on his waistcoat. "I'll visit the Bainbridges' table."

Ginger rose and smoothed out her lemon satin Schiaparelli gown.

Felicia pushed away from the table. "I'm coming with you." The amethyst gems of her headband sparkled in the light of the electric chandeliers. "Surely, you can't expect me to remain seated here on my own?" Her thin eyebrows arched high, and her cherry-red lips bowed. A crimson circle of rouge tinted her otherwise pale cheeks, and Ginger thought Felicia looked stunning, and certainly, where the earl was concerned, could give Poppy Kerslake a run for her money.

"You're welcome to join me," Ginger said.

Where Poppy stared at Ginger and Felicia with a stabbing glare, Lord Davenport-Witt's handsome face lit up with pleasure. Lionel Findley, on the other hand, looked bored and even checked his watch for the time.

"Good evening, Mrs. Reed, Miss Gold," Lord Davenport-Witt said. "So nice of you to join us." He lit a cigarette and placed a shiny silver lighter on the tablecloth beside the ashtray.

"We've only come to say hello," Ginger said.

Poppy tilted her head and huffed. "You mean you've come to interrogate us some more. Why are you wasting your time with us? We all loved Austin. The real killer isn't in this room."

"You seem awfully sure of that," Felicia said.

Ginger gave Felicia a sideways glance, then added, "I'm sure you're right, Miss Kerslake. The police are doing everything they can to find out who harmed Mr. Austin Bainbridge."

Poppy smirked. "Yeah, but are they any good?"

"They're investing all their best resources in the case," Ginger said lightly. "Which reminds me, do any of you know about a diamond mine in South Africa that was of interest to Mr. Bainbridge? I've heard he meant to invest."

Lionel Findley choked on his drink. "How did you

find out about that? An actual transaction never even took place."

Ginger smiled but let her gaze slip to Poppy. "The police have their ways."

THE TENSION AT THE BAINBRIDGES' table notched up as Basil strolled towards them. "Good evening," he said with a nod of his head. "How was the menu tonight?"

"The food was acceptable," Quentin said. "It wasn't like we had a lot of choice with the nasty weather brewing outside. I imagine you like to keep tabs on our lot anyway."

Basil's cheek tugged up on one side. The weather had been an inconvenience when he was merely a holi-daymaker, but now, as a detective, it was working in his favour.

"I'm sure we'd all like to get to the bottom of your brother's case as soon as possible."

Adeline Bainbridge worked the cloth napkin between her fingers as her eyes remained cast down-ward. Little Reggie kicked his legs and was in the process of sliding under the table.

"And how's it coming along?" Quentin said, then to his son he snapped, "Reggie! Sit up and sit still!"

Reggie whimpered and pulled himself back onto his chair. "Can we go now? I'm bored."

Basil held in a breath of impatience. "Mrs. Bainbridge, I would very much like to speak to you at your convenience. Perhaps I could call on you in your suite in an hour?"

"That won't do," Quentin said. "My wife is in a delicate condition and needs to sleep."

Basil would ask what he wanted to know here and now if it weren't for the boy. "Very well, tomorrow morning, then?"

Adeline Bainbridge offered a sharp nod of assent then pushed away from the table. "I'm dreadfully fatigued, and my little boy is restless." She turned to her husband. "You don't mind if I leave you to finish things here?"

"Go on," Quentin said. "I'll be up shortly."

With Adeline and Reggie gone, Basil pulled up an empty chair. "Why don't you want me to question your wife, Mr. Bainbridge?"

"I told you, she's in a delicate condition."

"Ah, but you see, my wife is as well—not so far along that one can notice—yet as you can see, she's perfectly capable of everyday social interaction." The men's gazes moved across the room to where Ginger interacted with the other table. Her poise and grace were evident, and Basil felt a swelling sense of pride.

He'd never stop thanking heaven that Ginger had agreed to be his wife.

"I'm afraid my wife is more fragile than most," Quentin said stiffly.

"It can't be avoided forever. I will speak to her, and I will get the truth from her, even if it has to be under oath in court."

It was a threat Basil hoped he wouldn't have to go through with. He was pleased to see Quentin blanch at the suggestion.

"What is your wife afraid of, Mr. Bainbridge?"

Quentin lifted a glass with a finger width of amber liquid remaining in it and slugged it back. After a hot breath, he said, "I got involved with another woman."

Basil kept his expression blank. Quentin's admission was hardly unique. His eyes darted to the earl's table, and Basil understood the source of Adeline's distress.

"Miss Kerslake," he stated.

"Yes. I had a flirtation with another woman, but Adeline can't see past it."

"When did this indiscretion happen?"

"Friday, shortly after we arrived. Austin's disappearance was yet to be taken seriously, and I thought her affections had turned from Austin to me."

"And your wife caught you in the act?"

"It sounds so lewd when you say it that way. We

were in the corridor. I thought she wanted. . . me. I pulled her in for a kiss, but Poppy pushed me away and slapped me. Adeline saw it all."

"What happened next?"

"Adeline jumped in the lift and headed downstairs, Poppy took the stairs, and I went back to our suite."

That would explain the emotional reaction Adeline Bainbridge had at seeing Poppy as she came down the stairs on the day that Ginger and Basil himself had arrived.

Quentin continued, "I couldn't chase Adeline without taking the stairs too; besides, Reggie was alone. It was all just a stupid mix up."

"Mr. Bainbridge, did you kill your brother so you could have his girl?"

"No, Chief Inspector, I did not. I might be a worm of a man, and unworthy of my wife's respect and affections, but I'm not a murderer."

Basil caught sight of Ginger, who'd returned to their table and looked over at him in expectation.

"Please do not leave this hotel, Mr. Bainbridge. If you do, I'll have you arrested for non-compliance. I'm afraid I will have to speak to Mrs. Bainbridge in the morning, but I'll ask my wife to accompany me. I promise we'll be kind."

Quentin Bainbridge lifted his glass to his lips then

swore when he found it empty. He waved his arm at the passing waiter. "Get me another!"

Felicia cast a dark look Miss Kerslake's way then excused herself. "I'm going to powder my nose."

"Don't dally," Ginger said lightly. "We may order dessert."

Felicia muttered, "Nothing for me, thank you."

"Poor dear," Ginger said, once she and Basil were alone. "She's not used to being second fiddle."

"I'm staying out of it."

Ginger grinned. "I know, I know, unless there's fire or blood, you'll not touch Felicia's love life with a ten-foot pole."

"Exactly."

Felicia's absence gave Ginger and Basil opportunity to share notes, and Ginger couldn't hold in her dismay when Basil told her about Quentin Bainbridge's indiscretion with Miss Kerslake.

"She's a siren!" Ginger said. "I'm afraid Felicia doesn't stand a chance."

Felicia returned at that moment, but Miss Kerslake had caught her attention, and Ginger was relieved Felicia hadn't overheard her last statement. The waiter provided a new diversion by bringing the apple and rice pudding Basil had ordered for them.

Mr. Findley leaving the Bainbridge party resulted in Felicia spending more time angrily sipping her glass of sherry as she tried in vain not to watch Lord Davenport-Witt and Miss Kerslake, who now dined alone together as if they were a perfectly attractive and charismatic couple.

Ginger patted Felicia's arm. "Perhaps he's not the one for you, Felicia."

"But I thought he liked me."

"I'm sure he does," Ginger said. Felicia was an appealing example of a bright young thing, which men like Lord Davenport-Witt found delightful. "But he seems rather, uh, undecided."

Felicia scowled.

Ginger glanced at Basil, who lifted a shoulder as he placed his spoon into his pudding.

The storm outside had turned into an ugly monster, which apparently matched the mood of Mr. Quentin Bainbridge. He threw back his drink as soon as the poor waiter had delivered it then hurried out of the restaurant. Lord Davenport-Witt and Miss Kerslake stood to leave shortly afterwards. The earl adeptly avoided the starlet's arm, which she'd held out before letting it drop when he didn't take it.

Ginger clucked her tongue. *So uncouth of the earl.* He nodded at their table, catching Felicia's eye for a moment longer than Ginger thought appropriate, before sauntering out. Allowing a moment of charity, she wondered if perhaps Miss Kerslake had a hold over

Lord Davenport-Witt that went beyond physical attraction. Poppy Kerslake proved unscrupulous when it came to going after what she wanted, even if it meant interfering in a man's marriage. Could she have Lord Davenport-Witt entangled in another way? Blackmail, perhaps?

The wind howled through the street-facing windows, and thunder rolled. The electric lights flickered before going out, leaving only the few table candles to cast light.

A scream followed, causing the hairs on the back of Ginger's neck to bristle. Basil picked up the candle as the trio rushed into the darkness of the hotel lobby.

A body lay at the foot of the stairs. In the eerie glow of candlelight, Ginger could see the lifeless form of Miss Kerslake lying at the foot of the staircase.

The electric lights snapped back on, and Ginger took in the stunned observers. At the top of the stairs stood Mrs. Merrick and Adeline Bainbridge, both with aghast expressions and fingers over open mouths.

In the lobby, Mr. Floyd ran out from his place behind the front desk, Mr. Bainbridge stepped out of the gents, and Lord Davenport-Witt made an entrance from the lift, the doors of which had remained opened. The earl's eyes darted from person to person, hitting Ginger just before falling to Poppy Kerslake lying on the floor.

"What the deuce!" Lord Davenport-Witt ran to the foot of the staircase, stopping short of the body. "Is she . . .?"

"Mr. Floyd," Ginger said. "Please call the doctor."

Quentin knelt beside Poppy Kerslake and lifted her wrist. "Poppy, dear, are you all right? Come on. Snap out of it, dear."

He glanced up at the startled faces of the onlookers. "Surely, she's simply unconscious." He leaned in to listen to Poppy's breath. "Poppy?"

Ginger glanced at Basil and shook her head subtly.

Basil took hold of the man's elbow. "The doctor will be here shortly."

Mr. Findley made a late appearance and joined the ladies who remained at the top of the stairs. Adeline Bainbridge stared at her husband with a look of fury, and Ginger guessed she wasn't happy about his public display of affection for Poppy Kerslake.

"What's all the racket about?" Mr. Findley asked.

"It's Miss Kerslake," Adeline said. "She's fallen down the stairs."

"She must have stumbled in the dark," Mrs. Merrick added. "Poor dear."

The wait for the doctor's arrival seemed interminable with a tangible sense of nervous tension and a growing dread as Poppy Kerslake's complexion grew ashen.

When the doctor finally arrived, a collective gasp was released. "I'm afraid this lady is dead," he immediately determined.

Basil addressed everyone with authority. "Until the

police and the medical examiner have had a chance to examine the situation, I must ask everyone to return to their rooms."

"Just retrieving my lighter, old chap," Lord Davenport-Witt said sombrely. "I left it at my table in the restaurant. Will only be a moment."

Quentin Bainbridge made quick strides to the lift and disappeared behind the bronze, grated doors. Ginger glanced at the landing; both ladies were gone. Mr. Findley's eyes narrowed as he stared at the twisted body of Poppy Kerslake before sharpening his grimace. When his gaze caught Ginger's, he made a quick pivot and marched down the corridor back towards his room.

Lord Davenport-Witt returned from the restaurant and made a show of producing his silver lighter. He paused at Felicia's side and frowned appropriately. "Such a shame. She was a real talent."

"Forgive my impertinence," Basil said. "You don't seem too upset."

"I'm terribly distraught, my good fellow. I'm not one to wear my emotions on my sleeve."

Mr. Floyd wrung his hands. "This is terrible. Simply terrible. The second disaster at this hotel in a fortnight. It will be dreadful for business!"

"Or good," Felicia said. "People are drawn to the morbid."

"Felicia darling," Ginger said. "You should probably go back to your suite too. The police will be here soon, and the fewer of us to get in the way, the better."

Lord Davenport-Witt held out an arm. "Might I escort you, Miss Gold."

Despite the gruesome circumstances, Felicia ducked her chin and allowed for a slight smile. "I'd be delighted."

Ginger caught Basil rolling his eyes.

The sound of clamouring bells grew increasingly louder, announcing the arrival of the Brighton Police. Soon afterwards, Detective Inspector Attwood and Constable Clarke marched in. After stamping his feet and shaking rain off his helmet, Detective Inspector Attwood stared at Basil. "Another body, sir?"

"I'm afraid so. Miss Poppy Kerslake had a bad fall down the stairs."

"Oh dear," Detective Inspector Attwood said. "I do love her films."

With a catch to his voice, Constable Clarke added, "Me too."

Detective Inspector Attwood circled the body, his lips tight as he took in the unnatural angle of Miss Kerslake's neck. "The medical examiner will be here soon. Clarke, snap a few photographs in the meantime."

"Yes, sir."

Constable Clarke rushed outside, presumably to collect the camera equipment.

"Do you know what happened?" Detective Inspector Attwood asked.

"We were dining in the restaurant when the lights went out."

"From the storm?"

"I'm presuming. Soon after, we heard a scream. Using the lit candle from our table, we came to the lobby and found Miss Kerslake lying here."

The detective inspector mused aloud, "Stumbled in the dark. An unfortunate accident."

Perhaps, in normal circumstances, Ginger would have been inclined to jump to that conclusion, but when the fallen was a prime suspect in a murder enquiry, she found the coincidence a mite *coincidental*. She turned to Basil. "Perhaps we shouldn't be too hasty?"

"Quite right," Basil said. "Miss Kerslake was a person of interest in the Austin Bainbridge case. I'd like to rule out foul play."

"Very well, sir," Detective Inspector Attwood said. "I'll get the forensic team to come in."

Dr. Johnstone arrived, his spectacles fogged up from the rain. He took a moment to wipe them with his handkerchief before carrying his black bag to the scene.

"Nasty fall, I see," he said.

"Is it possible to tell from what height she stumbled?" Ginger asked. "Had she made it to the top, or only partway?"

The medical examiner scanned the length of the staircase. "My guess would be from the top. A stumble from partway would certainly account for injuries, but the subject would have a better chance of stopping or slowing momentum. The further up the fall started, the more difficult it would have been for one to break one's fall."

He knelt, lifted Poppy's head, and found a bloody gash had sliced her scalp. He frowned deeply. "I'd say she fell backwards in a manner that would cause her to strike her head."

Basil climbed the stairs, slowing as he came to a spot on the wooden edge of the staircase. "Looks like blood. I'd surmise she hit her head here."

The doctor frowned. "Normally, if one loses one's footing, one falls forward and begins to slip. A tumble like this, resulting in the striking of one's head in that location, is unlikely unless one were inebriated or—"

Ginger filled in for him. "Pushed?"

Dr. Johnstone blew out his cheeks. "Lesions on her face would support the hypothesis. Her fall was dramatic."

.   .   .

WHILE BASIL KEPT a keen eye on Dr. Johnstone and the potential crime scene, Ginger meandered to the front desk, where Mr. Floyd stood with slumped shoulders. Dark circles ringed the manager's eyes, and the smile of servitude he gave Ginger looked forced.

With a tone of weariness, he asked, "Can I assist you with anything, madam?"

"No, I just thought I should step out of the way. Not a pleasant evening, now, is it?"

"No, madam."

"Might I ask, Mr. Floyd, how well do you know Mrs. Merrick?"

Mr. Floyd's pencil-thin moustache quivered. "Quite well. We're cousins, in fact. Why do you ask?"

"Oh, just curious. And the owners of this hotel, where are they?"

"The Winthrops set up permanent residency in New York City. They only pop in once a year or so." He collapsed a little into himself. "I dread having to share this new bit of bad news."

"Does the Winthrop family leave the running of the hotel to you and Mrs. Merrick, then?"

"Yes, madam." He sighed. "We never had any problems before this lot came."

Ginger ducked her chin. "Rather bad luck for both you and them."

The forensic team had arrived. Ginger left the

manager and rejoined Basil, who had remained on watch.

Basil nodded towards the front desk. "Anything of interest?"

"Did you know that Mr. Floyd and Mrs. Merrick were related?"

"I did not."

"Cousins."

"How interesting."

Detective Inspector Attwood called for Basil's attention. "Palm print on the wall on the landing about six feet from the stairs. Looks to belong to the victim. You can see that she has a scar on the palm of her hand —a unique identifier. The same print is on the wall."

"One might hold the railing when going up the stairs," Ginger said, "but a lady wouldn't palm the wall like that unless she'd lost her balance."

"Miss Kerslake was poise itself," Constable Clarke said, a hitch evident in his voice.

"Indeed," Basil said. "It indicates that Miss Kerslake had a physical encounter on the landing."

Ginger nodded. "And that she was pushed down the stairs."

Basil stared at Detective Inspector Attwood. "I'm calling this murder, Detective Inspector. Please ensure that none of the witnesses leave the hotel."

"Yes, sir," Detective Inspector Attwood said, then

to Constable Clarke. "Confirm the room numbers from the manager and knock on doors to make sure everyone is where they should be."

Ginger sidled up beside Basil. "Ten to one Poppy Kerslake's death is related to Austin Bainbridge's."

Basil agreed. "We find the killer for one, and we'll find the killer for two."

Constable Clarke returned a few minutes later. "Everyone is in their rooms and promises to remain there for the night, sir."

"Very good," Basil said.

Dr. Johnstone reported the completion of his initial examination. "I presume that the deceased died from a broken neck. An autopsy will confirm that definitively. If you're ready, the body can be removed."

"You may proceed," Basil said.

"Where shall we start?" Ginger asked. "With the ladies on the landing?" Ginger thought one or both had arrived at the scene rather quickly.

"Let's have a go at the Bainbridges," Basil said. "Get two out of the way in one sitting."

Ginger popped into her suite to freshen up and collect Boss. The little dog stared at her with round brown eyes, and an enthusiastic stubby wag of his tail.

"Oh, Bossy. You can come along to the interviews." She cast a glance at Basil. "It's all right, love, isn't it?"

"I'm sure it can't hurt."

"He'll be so well behaved, I promise," Ginger said as she scooped him into her arms. "Won't you, Boss?"

Quentin Bainbridge's scowl was deep and dark when he opened the door to Basil's knock. Ginger didn't know if it was the effect of too much whisky or a guilty conscience.

"We won't be long," Basil said. "May we come in?"

It wasn't a request, and Quentin knew it. "Let's just get the bloody thing over with."

Ginger took a seat in a chair next to Adeline Bainbridge, who sat forlornly, working a handkerchief with her fingers. She scowled at the presence of Boss on Ginger's lap but said nothing, apparently choosing her battles.

Hoping to put the lady at ease, Ginger smiled. "I hope you don't mind. I have my little dog with me. He is well behaved."

Quentin topped off a crystal glass with another shot of whisky and lifted his glass in the air. "Can I interest you in a nightcap, Chief Inspector?"

"Thank you, but I'm on duty at the moment."

"Suit yourself." Quentin slumped into a chair. "I don't see what all the fuss is about. Sadly, Poppy lost her footing when the lights went out. Doesn't seem like a big mystery to me."

Basil took the remaining chair. "I'm afraid it's more complicated than that. The evidence suggests someone pushed Miss Kerslake."

Adeline Bainbridge gasped, pressing her handkerchief to her mouth. "No. Not another one."

"We're looking to establish the whereabouts of all the guests at the time of Miss Kerslake's fall, Mrs. Bainbridge," Ginger said.

"I was here, putting Reggie to bed. I ran into the corridor when I heard Miss Kerslake scream."

"You ran out in the dark?" Ginger said.

"Well, when the lights went out as I happened to be walking by the door, I fumbled to find the handle then opened it. The corridor was black, and I couldn't see anything until my eyes adjusted."

Basil jotted notes in his notebook, then glanced over at Quentin. "What about you, Mr. Bainbridge?"

"I hadn't even made it upstairs. Nature called, and I made use of the ground-floor facilities. Believe me, it was a right nuisance when the lights went out in the middle of things."

"Just to confirm," Basil started, "you never went upstairs before the lights went out."

Quentin responded with a note of belligerence, "You saw me leave the restaurant."

"Yes, and you'd have had plenty of time to run up the stairs, push Miss Kerslake, and return down the staff staircase."

After blowing a loud raspberry, Quentin said, "That's preposterous. Why would I bother?"

Ginger answered. "Perhaps you didn't like the attention Miss Kerslake gives Lord Davenport-Witt?"

Quentin stared back with fire in his eyes. "Why would I care about that?"

"Is it not true that you and Miss Kerslake had a dalliance?"

Quentin glared at his wife, who studiously studied her hands.

"That was a one-time mistake. Which I've apologised for a thousand times, and a mishap for which I will apparently never be forgiven."

Ginger wondered if Adeline had seen a serendipitous opportunity to rid herself of a threat and taken it? She didn't think they'd get the truth out of her with her drunk and angry husband in the room. She looked over at Basil with a nod of her head.

"Perhaps we'll resume our interview in the morning," Basil said. "We'll all be better off after a good night's sleep."

Neither of the Bainbridges bothered to see them out.

Ginger set Boss on the carpet of the corridor, and

he sat obediently, waiting for his next command. Ginger posed her question to Basil instead. "Where to now?"

"Lord Davenport-Witt was the last to see her alive," Basil said, "at least from what we know."

Ginger tilted her head towards the earl's door, and Basil stepped beside her. He knocked, and Lord Davenport-Witt quickly opened it. "Ah, I expected to see you tonight, Chief Inspector. Mrs. Reed, a pleasant surprise."

"Not really a surprise, I'm sure," Ginger said as she strolled into the gentleman's room, which smelled sharply of cigar smoke. She was surprised to see Mr. Findley there. He nodded and tapped ashes into an ashtray.

"I see you've decided to console each other on your loss together," Basil said.

"We've all suffered a second, dreadful shock," Lord Davenport-Witt said. "You can't blame us fellows for wanting to share a drink or two."

"I welcome the convenience," Basil said, though Ginger could tell he wasn't happy that two suspects were potentially colluding with each other.

"You don't mind if I bring my dog in," Ginger said. "He's very well behaved. You won't even notice he's here."

"Not at all," Lord Davenport-Witt said. He took a

moment to pat Boss on the head. "I'm a dog person myself."

Mr. Findley let out an exaggerated breath. "Can we get on with it."

"We just have a few questions," Basil said.

After a drag on his cigar, Mr. Findley said, "I have to admit that this is getting rather tiresome."

"Murder is such a blot on one's plans," Ginger said.

Mr. Findley's brows jumped. "Murder? I thought you wanted to talk about Miss Kerslake, not Austin."

"We do," Ginger said. "Evidence indicates that Miss Kerslake was pushed."

"Oh, bloody hell." After another exaggerated sigh, Mr. Findley muttered, "I knew that woman was trouble from the moment I met her."

"Which was when?" Basil asked.

"Last summer, at a house party, she was Austin's latest female acquisition. I honestly didn't think she'd be around as long as she was, but she was the first famous actress Austin had met, so the novelty lasted longer than most."

"You didn't like Miss Kerslake much, Mr. Findley," Basil said.

Mr. Findley snorted. "She was a troublemaker, but I didn't push her down the stairs."

"Where were you when she fell?" Ginger asked.

"In my room." He removed a thin volume from his

jacket pocket—*The Great Impersonation.* "Reading this."

Ginger was familiar with the popular Great War spy thriller.

"I find fictional characters more to my liking than real ones, who are a pain in the derrière. The fact that I'm being held hostage in this hotel is evidence of that."

Lord Davenport-Witt stubbed out his cigar, causing a plume of blue to rise to the ceiling. "You're rather hard on the rest of us, old chap."

Mr. Findley scowled in return then looked off into the distance.

"Where were you, Lord Davenport-Witt, when Miss Kerslake took her tumble?" Basil asked.

"I had just stepped into the lift. But the electricity went off before I could push the button."

"I didn't see the attendant, Mr. Weaver, tonight," Ginger said.

"No. The lift was empty, but that's not uncommon for late evenings, and especially with so few guests. It's not as if we can't push a button on our own."

Or, Ginger thought, Lord Davenport-Witt could've pushed Miss Kerslake. When the lights went back on, the earl could have quickly taken the staff stairs down one floor and stepped inside the main lift as a dramatic presentation to establish an alibi. But why would he want Poppy dead? Ginger couldn't think of a motive.

19

When Ginger took Boss out for his walk the next morning, she was pleased to see that the storm had passed. Even though the sky was grey, a glow of light on the horizon over the sea promised better weather to come. Seabirds circled overhead as the waves lapped the shore and stained the pebbly beach in dark curvy lines. People, once again, were out and about, breathing in the damp, saline air.

As she headed back along the promenade, she could see the familiar figure of Adeline Bainbridge standing on the pebbly beach, her arms crossed against the cold. The way Adeline watched the waves crash to shore with a sense of longing on her face made Ginger's heart tighten. Her stance highlighted the fact that new life was bursting inside her.

"Come, Boss," Ginger said, picking up her pace.

"Let's catch Mrs. Bainbridge before she goes back inside." Or, before she did something dreadful that Ginger certainly didn't want to witness.

She called out, "Mrs. Bainbridge!"

As if she'd been pulled out of a dream, Adeline slowly turned her gaze towards Ginger. "Good morning, Mrs. Reed."

"Good morning. A bit of a blustery day, isn't it?"

"Yes, I suppose."

"It hasn't been a good time these last few days," Ginger said. "First, finding Mr. Bainbridge's body and then Poppy dying."

"You're stating the obvious," Adeline said stiffly. "Please don't beat around the bush. What do you want to say to me?"

"Very well. Did you push Miss Kerslake down the stairs?"

"I did not. But that's not to say I'm sorry for her. She caused my family a lot of grief."

"How so?"

Adeline faced Ginger and held her gaze. "Your husband seems very devoted to you."

"Yes. We're devoted to each other."

"You're fortunate. Not all women can say the same." She inhaled the saline air, letting it escape slowly through her lips. "When Austin came to our London home with Poppy Kerslake on his arm,

Quentin was immediately smitten. He tried to hide it from me, to spare my feelings, I suppose, but he's not an actor, and everyone could tell he was in love with her." A sad smile crossed her lips. "It was terribly humiliating. Quentin hurt me, so I wanted to hurt him."

By pushing Poppy down the stairs?

"How so?" Ginger asked.

Adeline ran her hand, red from the cold, over her bulging stomach. "This is Austin's. Austin always wanted what he couldn't have, which included me. Except, one night, I let him have it."

Oh mercy.

"Does your husband know?"

"No. When it came time to use my ammunition against Quentin my fury had faded and I'd lost my courage. Nothing good would come from either brother learning the truth."

Ginger couldn't help but feel sorry for Mrs. Bainbridge. "What are you going to do now?" she asked.

"I'm trapped, aren't I? I have Reggie to think about, and this baby needs a father. As far as everyone is concerned, Quentin is the father. It's a difficult situation for everyone when you've fallen out of love."

inger followed Adeline—who walked briskly, staying an unfriendly distance ahead of Ginger—back to the hotel. Clearly, she didn't long for Ginger's company, so Ginger held back in the lobby, allowing Adeline to take a solo trip in the lift.

Boss sniffed the carpet, and Ginger wondered how many strange and intriguing scents lingered there—enough to capture the attention of her pet, at any rate. Changing her mind about waiting for the lift, she headed for the staircase, where a familiar giggle echoed down.

Felicia descended the long staircase with Lord Davenport-Witt beside her. They were an attractive set, and under other circumstances, Ginger might feel a twinge of hope and happiness for Felicia. As it was, their seemingly carefree descent over the scene of Poppy Kerslake's recent demise seemed heartless.

"Oh, good morning, Ginger!" Felicia said when she spotted her.

"Good morning, Felicia. Lord Davenport-Witt."

The earl had the decency to erase the joy from his face as they reached the lobby. "Good morning, Mrs. Reed. I hope you slept well after such a horrible event."

"Well enough," Ginger said. "And you?"

"Not very well. Poppy was a friend, a bubbly personality, and it was such a shock to see her life end so dramatically."

Ginger hummed. From what she'd been gleaning about Miss Kerslake's life, no man was merely a *friend*.

"Lord Davenport-Witt and I met in the corridor, quite serendipitously,"

Felicia certainly said that a little too eagerly, Ginger thought.

"We're heading to the restaurant for breakfast," Felicia continued. "Would you like to join us?"

Ginger knew Felicia. She could hear in Felicia's tone and see in the blankness of her well-made-up eyes that the invitation was a pleasantry only—Felicia's true desire was to breakfast alone with the earl.

How can I allow that when Lord Davenport-Witt could be a killer? Even though she'd already eaten breakfast in their suite, she smiled and said, "I'd be delighted. Allow me to take Boss back to my suite and fetch Basil. We'll see you soon."

The bell for the lift rang, and Ginger stepped in. Mr. Weaver hadn't returned to work, so Ginger closed the grate and pushed the button for her floor.

"I don't know what it is about that man, Bossy," Ginger said as she held him under one arm, "but I don't trust him."

An empty breakfast tray and yesterday's newspaper lay on the floor in front of Mr. Findley's room, and Ginger could only assume that Lionel Findley chose to remain inside.

"There you are," Basil said, as Ginger and Boss returned to their suite.

"Our walk took a little longer than planned," Ginger said. "I ran into Felicia. She's with Lord Davenport-Witt and is quite blinded by his charm."

"You really don't like the fellow, do you?"

"It's not that. I just have a feeling he's hiding something. Perhaps bigger than the case here."

Basil's hazel eyes glimmered with affection. "I trust your intuition, love. What do you want to do?"

"What I want is to keep Felicia away from him, but I can't exactly forbid her from seeing him without reason. She believes in his innocence, wholeheartedly."

"He's innocent until proved guilty."

"Oh, I know but . . ." Ginger drew her fingers

through the air. "They're waiting for us. We're joining them for breakfast."

Basil glanced at the empty food trolley next to their table. "After the breakfast we've just had, I'm quite full. And a maid brought me a message from Dr. Johnstone. He's asking us to come to the mortuary."

"Oh mercy. Well, that does sound important then." Ginger felt torn between her curiosity and her desire to protect her sister-in-law. "I suppose Felicia can't get into too much trouble while we're gone. So long as she doesn't leave the hotel." She smiled wryly, "And refrains from using the stairs."

Felicia was a little too pleased when Ginger expressed her regrets, and Ginger made a mental note to have a talk with her on her return.

After a short taxicab ride, Ginger and Basil arrived at the hospital and were directed to the mortuary. Dr. Johnstone was waiting.

"Good day, Chief Inspector, Mrs. Reed."

"Good day, Dr. Johnstone," Basil said. "What do you have for us?"

THROUGH THE WINDOW into the theatre, Ginger could see the body of Miss Kerslake covered with a sheet. A second table held the remains of Austin Bainbridge.

Catching Dr. Johnstone's eyes, she enquired, "What have you learned about Mr. Bainbridge and Miss Kerslake?"

"I can tell you that the cause of death for them both was a severed spinal cord in the neck area."

Ginger stared at Basil and said, "Another tumble down the stairs?"

"It's a probable cause."

"And Austin Bainbridge didn't have the convenience of a power cut to explain his fall," Ginger added, "so the killer had to do away with his body."

"Taking the largest trunk available, which happened to belong to Poppy Kerslake," Basil said, "but then what? It would take at least two people to lift Austin Bainbridge into the trunk."

Dr. Johnstone interjected, "And dead weight is considerably heavier. From the remains, I can deduce by height and mass that the deceased weighed around thirteen stone when alive."

"Is there anything else?" Basil said.

The medical examiner scanned his notes. "Nothing obvious. Miss Kerslake was in perfect health otherwise. Unfortunately, Mr. Bainbridge's body was too decomposed to determine much else."

Ginger and Basil thanked the doctor before leaving. The sun had broken through the clouds, though dark banks of threatening clouds continued to rest on the horizon. The couple welcomed the momentary warm breeze.

"Let's take a stroll along the promenade while the sun is out," Ginger suggested.

Basil agreed, and after a short taxicab ride, they exited at the Brighton Marine Palace and Pier. A new development to come out of the last century, this typical British pier, which extended over seventeen hundred feet into the English Channel, was an amusement park with merry-go-rounds, a Ferris wheel, and entertainment for the whole family. The theatre at its entrance was a popular venue for acts such as Stan Laurel and Charlie Chaplin.

Linking arms, they strolled amongst the holiday-makers eating biscuits and sipping fizzy drinks. Happy music sounded as they weaved between the merry-go-round and Ferris wheel.

"We really do have to come back with Scout sometime," Ginger said.

"Indeed," Basil agreed. "Perhaps by the end of the summer."

Ginger let out a breath of contentment and returned her mind to the case at hand. She loved a good puzzle. "Assuming one person was responsible for the initial push that resulted in Austin Bainbridge's death," she said, "the killer must have had an accomplice after the fact."

"Someone close enough to the killer who would want to protect him or her," Basil said. "Adeline and Quentin?"

"Or Poppy and another? Perhaps she was threatening to expose the killer."

"She'd expose herself then."

"Not if she denied it. Or perhaps she thought she'd get away with it because of her charm. A good scandal can do wonders for a lagging career."

Basil stopped a food vendor selling fish and chips. "Are you hungry?"

She was, but the strong smell of grease unsettled her stomach.

"There's a teashop near the hotel," Ginger said. "Do you mind if we eat there? I fancy a bun."

"Sounds wonderful," Basil said.

The teashop had rustic wooden-beamed ceilings and white plaster walls. Shelving units sat along the perimeter, crowded with teapots and tea settings available for purchase. Wooden tables and ladder-back chairs dotted the floors. The ambience was inviting, with warm lighting and the cheerful chatter of happy patrons.

They placed their orders of tea and salmon and cucumber sandwiches. A pleasant-faced waitress, who appeared to enjoy her job, took their order.

Ginger forced herself to slow down, but the food

was simply delicious. Basil unsuccessfully tried to hold in a smile.

"What?" Ginger said.

"What? Can't I smile at my wife?"

Ginger tilted her head playfully. "It depends on why?"

Basil's grin broke into a full smile. "You're lovely, that's all."

"Oh, you're just a big flirt."

Ginger raised a triangle of a sandwich to her mouth to take another bite, but before the savoury goodness touched her lips, the door opened, and Lionel Findley strolled in.

Basil followed her gaze. "Shall we invite Mr. Findley to join us?"

"Of course."

Ginger's mind created new possible pairings of who might be involved in the death of Austin Bainbridge: Lionel Findley and Poppy Kerslake. Lionel Findley and either of the remaining Bainbridges. Mr. Findley and Quentin Bainbridge both found Austin Bainbridge a financial hurdle. While either Poppy or Adeline might have pushed Austin in a fit of passion, Lionel might've cavalierly helped either lady to cover the crime.

She waved an arm and smiled, "Mr. Findley, hello!"

Lionel Findley's expression soured when he spotted her and Basil in the shop, and Ginger didn't doubt he would've turned and walked out if propriety hadn't dictated otherwise. Basil motioned to the empty chair. "Do join us."

With reluctance, Mr. Findley removed his hat and took a seat. When the waitress came, he ordered tea, black.

"I knew Brighton was a small town," he said, "next to London, at any rate, but it seems that here one can't avoid anyone else who's tied up in this situation."

Ginger patted him on the arm. "It's fate, Mr. Findley. You'll be pleased to know that we've been informed of Austin's cause of death." She glanced at Basil, who nodded his consent to reveal.

"And what is that?"

"His neck was broken."

With a slight shaking of the hand, Lionel Findley took a sip of tea. "I'm sorry to hear it."

"We're theorising that, much like Miss Kerslake, Austin had a fall down the stairs."

Mr. Findley's eyes darkened as he stared back at her. "You mean *pushed*."

"Quite likely," Basil said. "And then his body was unceremoniously placed into Miss Kerslake's trunk and later deposited in the sea."

"A dreadful affair."

"Was it Miss Kerslake's idea to use her trunk?" Ginger asked. The starlet would've known the size of her trunk and that it would be large enough for the task at hand.

Mr. Findley's upper lip pulled back. "How would I know?"

"Perhaps you saw it happen?" Ginger said. "Perhaps you saw Poppy push Austin down the stairs then, when she pleaded for your help, assisted her in hiding the body?"

Mr. Findley pushed his unfinished tea aside and stood. "For detectives, the two of you aren't doing a very good job. I can assure you that I never saw who killed Austin, and I most certainly wouldn't have helped to cover it up if I had. I do hope you solve this thing soon, as I'm needed in London. Good day to you both."

As if he couldn't get away fast enough, Mr. Findley hurried to the door and stormed out of the tea shop. Ginger nibbled her lip and looked at Basil. "What do you think? Is he telling the truth?"

"I wouldn't know, love. I wouldn't know."

21

*G*inger couldn't help but notice that Mr. Cooper, the porter, was still not in his position, but wrote it off as being due to the shortage of guests. Instead, she and Basil were warmly greeted by Mr. Floyd, who, if one could go by the restlessness of his thin moustache, was eager to deliver some news.

"Daphne Love, the very talented jazz singer, has agreed to perform tonight. Dinner and dancing in the lounge starting at eight o'clock." He lowered his voice and spoke discreetly behind his hand, which he held to his lips. "We need to do something to bring the guests back, and fortunately, the storm is moving east. I'm anticipating better weather in the morning!"

Ginger couldn't fault the manager for his enthusiasm, and she did love a good dance, but the timing didn't feel right.

"Oh," he said, as if he could read her thoughts, "We mean no disrespect to the recently departed, but dancing will distract the people from yet another unfortunate event here at the hotel. As they say, the living have to keep on living."

Peeking inside the restaurant, Ginger was relieved that the table Felicia and Lord Davenport-Witt had occupied earlier was now empty. *Were the two still together? And if so, where?* The lounge had yet to open, and Ginger hadn't spotted them on the boardwalk or in front of the shops, but that didn't mean they hadn't gone out and she had simply missed seeing them.

Unlike the porter, Mr. Weaver had returned to operate the lift. "Good day, Chief Inspector and Mrs. Reed," he said.

Basil replied, "Good day, Mr. Weaver."

Mr. Weaver closed the grate doors and pushed a button. "I'm sorry to hear about Miss Kerslake's unfortunate demise. I remember when I first saw her, must be two years ago now. She had dark hair then, a natural beauty. Such a shock to think she's no longer with us."

"Did you say two years ago?" Ginger asked. Poppy Kerslake had given her the impression that this visit with the Bainbridge family was her first time to Brighton and the hotel.

"Yes. She was on the arm of another young man at that time. I imagine a lady like her has plenty of suitors."

"What month would that have been?" Basil asked.

"July. I remember because it was my birthday, and Miss Kerslake sang happy birthday to me." He smiled at the memory. "I think she'd had a little too much to drink."

The lift reached its destination, and Mr. Weaver opened the doors. "I wish you both a pleasant afternoon."

"Thank you, Mr. Weaver," Ginger said. "Oh, one question. Do you know the name of the gentleman that was with Miss Kerslake two years ago?"

Mr. Weaver's jolly countenance dimmed. "Perhaps you should ask Mr. Floyd."

Ginger wanted to press Mr. Weaver for answers, but the sound of Felicia and Lord Davenport-Witt's voices in the corridor distracted her, and when she turned back, the lift doors were closed.

Felicia's complexion was flush with excitement. "Oh, Ginger," she said when she spotted her. "Lord Davenport-Witt and I just had a marvellous jaunt on a catamaran!"

"Just the two of you?" Ginger said, feeling alarmed.

"We hardly needed a chaperone on a catamaran, Ginger. Besides, this is the twentieth century."

"That was rather forward," Basil said, giving the earl a disapproving stare.

The earl had the decency to look abashed. "I'm afraid it was rather impromptu," he said. "The weather was suddenly gorgeous, and the rental man appeared just as we were walking by."

"You're skilled with boats then," Ginger said. And could easily have taken a vessel out to dispose of the trunk with a body in it.

"We live on an island," the earl returned with a half-grin. "Sailing is a popular pastime, especially for the gentry."

"Indeed," Ginger said. "Good day, Lord Davenport-Witt." She placed her hand on Felicia's elbow and pushed her towards her suite.

"Ginger!" Felicia hissed.

Ginger forced a light tone. "Darling, I want to hear all about your adventures. I'm sure Lord Davenport-Witt understands you need a change of clothes. Look, your dress is stained with salt from the spray off the sea."

Basil unlocked the door to their suite, and Ginger guided Felicia inside. Boss, who'd been sleeping on one of the chairs, roused himself awake, stretched out his hind legs, and jumped to the floor to greet them.

"Hello, Bossy," Ginger said. "So sorry to leave you alone for so long."

"I'm going to my suite," Felicia said stiffly.

"How could you be so careless?" Ginger muttered, soothing her anxiety by scrubbing Boss' neck.

"What do you mean? I can swim if that's what you're worried about."

"I'm worried about the fact that you went out sailing with a suspected murderer!"

"Oh, dash it! Lord Davenport-Witt wouldn't hurt a mouse."

"And you know this, how?" Ginger asked. "Murderers don't always look like monsters that live under the bed."

Felicia appealed to Basil. "She's being unreasonable, isn't she?"

"I have to agree with my wife," Basil said. "This *is* a murder investigation."

"A double murder investigation," Ginger added. "We've just returned from the mortuary. Austin Bainbridge also died from a broken neck."

Felicia's voice cracked. "Also?"

"Yes. Miss Kerslake's fall down the staircase resulted in a fatal neck injury. It's quite possible that Mr. Bainbridge died the same way. This is not the time to be reckless with people you don't know, no matter how handsome and eligible."

"Fine, I get your point. And, as you so readily

pointed out, I must change my frock!" Felicia marched to the door and slammed it behind her.

Ginger fell into a chair with a sigh and rested her chin on Boss' head. "Oh mercy. Was I too hard on her?"

Basil stepped behind her and placed his warm hands on Ginger's shoulders, rubbing gently. "Felicia shouldn't have put you in a position where she required scolding. If the earl is our killer, then going out to sea alone without anyone knowing was a foolish thing for her to do, indeed."

Just the thought of what could've been caused Ginger's heart to constrict. She should've sent Felicia home with Ambrosia and Scout when she'd had the chance!

WHEN GINGER LAY down for a mid-afternoon nap, a luxury his wife had been taking advantage of since her pregnancy, Basil headed down to the lobby in search of Floyd. He couldn't help but feel the man was holding something back, which wasn't surprising since it was the manager's job, along with all the other employees of the hotel, to show a high level of discretion. This determination to keep the secrets of others made Basil's task more difficult. In most cases, finding people willing to gossip was easy, even if the teller's version of the truth was often suspect.

Floyd wasn't at his usual position behind the desk, but as fortune would have it, Cooper was in his uniform and stationed by the door. But before Basil could reach the lad, Quentin Bainbridge, with his long strides, breezed by. His chin was pointed down, and he didn't seem aware of those around him.

"Mr. Bainbridge," Basil called.

Quentin stopped suddenly, his expression growing dour as his eyes focused on Basil's approach.

"Oh, Chief Inspector Reed," he said with a short exhale.

"Might I have a minute?"

"Certainly, though I am in a hurry. Adeline is in desperate need of something sweet, and I promised her I'd quickly pop to the shops."

Basil waved the man out of hearing range of the porter.

"I hate to bring this up, Mr. Bainbridge, but it's come to my attention that your wife—forgive me, this is rather delicate—that your wife and your brother may have been, er, friendly."

Quentin's face turned the colour of undercooked beetroot. "How dare you suggest . . ?"

"Are you saying, the thought never occurred to you?"

Had Quentin suspected a dalliance between his wife and his brother? Perhaps he'd pushed the latter down the staircase in a moment of rage. And had Adeline, out of guilt, helped him to cover it up?

"O-o-of course not," Quentin stammered. "That's preposterous! How shameful for the constabulary and especially Scotland Yard to pay regard to tabloid rumours. Just leave my wife out of this!"

Bainbridge stormed outside like a bull, pushing the exterior doors wide before Cooper could do the honours.

"Good day, sir," the porter called out.

Basil, unfazed by Bainbridge's tumultuous exit, approached the porter. "Mr. Cooper, good to see you back. Is everything all right? You're feeling fine?"

Cooper's dark eyes darted to the desk before landing back on Basil—a forced smile following, and Basil had the distinct impression that he worried about Floyd seeing them speaking together.

"Yes, very fine, sir. Mr. Floyd gave me the day off because it was slow. Now with Miss Love performing tonight, things will be busy again."

"Indeed. You heard the sad news about Miss Kerslake."

Cooper's gaze moved to a spot over Basil's shoulder then fell to his polished black shoes. "Yes, sir. A terrible thing that was. She was a lovely lady."

"I've learned that she came to stay at the Brighton Seaside Hotel two years ago. Do you remember seeing her then?"

"I think that was before I worked here, sir." His eyes widened as his attention was drawn to something else. Basil followed the porter's gaze to the front desk and the reemergence of Floyd. Cooper turned from Basil and pretended to busy himself with the umbrella stand. Clearly, the porter had been warned against speaking to the police.

"Thank you, Mr. Cooper," Basil said. With a non-threatening smile on his face, he strolled casually, fists in his trouser pockets, towards the front desk.

"Ah, Chief Inspector Reed," Floyd began, "I hope everything is to your liking. Is there something that I can do for you or Mrs. Reed?"

"Just a few questions, if you don't mind. I'm afraid, with Miss Kerslake's death, I'm going to have to keep asking them for a while."

"Certainly," Floyd said without enthusiasm. "Such a terrible accident. Anything I can do to help the police."

"First, I'm afraid to have to tell you that Miss Kerslake's fall was unlikely an accident."

The manager's long fingers trembled as he reached for his collar. "What are you saying? That she was, er, pushed?"

"It appears that way. It's my understanding that Miss Kerslake had been a guest here two years ago."

Floyd swallowed. "It's possible. I don't remember every guest and the time of their reservation."

Basil ignored the manager's lie. Floyd was the epitome of observation and detail recollection.

"She either arrived with a gentleman or met one whilst she was here. Do you recall the man?"

"As I said, I can't possibly be expected to remember every guest."

"But it would be recorded in your ledger, would it not?" Basil tapped the open registration book with his finger. "Please have a look at your entries in the year of 1924, Mr. Floyd, or if you prefer, I can get a warrant."

Floyd threw up both palms in protest. "That will not be necessary. Please, give me a moment to look. Do you have a month in mind?"

"July."

"Yes, well, let me see."

Floyd flipped through the pages of the register rather slowly, Basil thought. He drew his finger down each page as if he had to silently read each entry to ensure the name written there was not Miss Kerslake. If the manager thought Basil would tire of waiting, he was mistaken.

Finally, he landed on her name. "Yes, she registered on the fifth."

"Did a gentleman register at the same time."

"Yes, sir, but I doubt they were together—one registered after the other."

"Who was the man?"

"Please forgive me sir, but I do think you're on the wrong path."

Basil tightened his jaw in frustration. "The name, Mr. Floyd."

Floyd swallowed again. "John Merrick, sir."

"Merrick? A relation of the housekeeper?"

"Er, I couldn't say, sir."

22

The lounge had been reoriented with tables moved to the edges and extra ambient lighting helped to create a relaxed atmosphere. Ginger felt it would be excusable if one didn't recognise the room.

The ladies, in colours as bright as spring flora, wore a variation of smooth, mid-calf gowns with bare shoulders, long white gloves, and the odd feather embellishment. Wearing black three-piece suits, some even with coat-tails and top hats, the gentlemen came into the room looking well-groomed and debonair.

Not all were guests of the hotel, but such a distinction didn't keep them from spending money on fancy drinks and cigarettes. If one didn't know about the tragic events attached to this hotel, the evening's festivities certainly didn't point to them.

Looking every bit the sultry jazz singer Daphne Love aspired to be, she wore a glittering white gown that swooped low down her back. The band upped the tempo, and Ginger and Basil stole the show—as they often did when dancing—showing off the quick steps of the Charleston. Dancing had first brought Ginger and Basil together, what seemed like eons ago aboard the SS *Rosa,* sailing from Boston to England a year after her father died

So much had happened since then! Ginger and Basil had met Scout on that ship. Who would've dreamt she and Basil would one day marry and adopt the lad? Ginger had come to England to claim part of her inheritance, Hartigan House, in South Kensington. Her father also had large stakes in several successful businesses in America. After she had decided to stay in London, she opened her fashion boutique, Feathers & Flair. Since then, she'd established the office of Lady Gold Investigations.

No wonder I'm constantly tired, Ginger thought, feeling ready to leave the dance floor.

The song ended, and Basil guided her back to their table. Ginger used her lace handkerchief to dab her moist forehead. "Such marvellous fun, but I'm feeling rather overheated."

"I'll get you a drink," Basil said. "Another Coca-Cola?"

"Yes, thank you, love," Ginger said. "You're a brick."

Sitting with a straight back, Felicia crossed and exposed her pale leg. She tapped long, painted fingernails against her glass.

"Is everything all right?" Ginger asked.

"Huh?"

A new song started up, making it difficult to hear casual conversation across the table. Ginger leaned closer. "Are you all right?"

"Yes, of course, why wouldn't I be?"

Ginger considered her sister-in-law, who was clearly still upset with the talking-to she'd been given her earlier. Ginger glanced up at the stranger who had approached their table.

"Might I have the pleasure of this dance?" he asked.

He'd smiled politely at Ginger, but his eyes focused on Felicia. With a nod of her head, Ginger encouraged her. The fellow seemed nice enough. At least, it wasn't Lord Davenport-Witt, who hadn't yet bothered to make an appearance. Felicia smiled politely and accepted.

Basil returned with the promised drink, and Ginger sipped it gratefully.

"That certainly hits the spot."

Basil took the empty seat beside her and grunted.

"Dancing with you is great fun, but I can't help feeling that I'm wasting valuable time."

"Have you heard anything more from Detective Inspector Attwood or Dr. Johnstone?" Ginger had slept for a shockingly long time that afternoon, and with dressing and preparing for the evening's festivities hadn't had a chance to review the case. As it was, her stomach protested, and she was quite ready for the dinner portion of the evening to begin.

"No, but I did learn something interesting from Mr. Floyd. A John Merrick registered immediately after Miss Kerslake on the fifth of July 1924."

Ginger's thinly plucked brows arched dramatically. "The same last name as the housekeeper?"

"Mr. Floyd denies that he's a relation."

"Could be a coincidence."

Ginger scanned the dance floor for Felicia. Her tangerine, Egyptian-style gown was easy to spot, but the gentleman in whose arms she was dancing wasn't the stranger that had approached them. Instead, she swayed with a rather debonair-looking Lord Davenport-Witt.

Ginger sniffed. "I hoped that he'd refrain from attending."

"Better here where we can monitor him than him getting into mischief elsewhere," Basil said.

"I'd hope he'd get into mischief with someone else."

Ginger smiled. "You don't mind if I cut in on her, do you?"

"You want to dance with Lord Davenport-Witt?"

"Perhaps he'll let something important slip."

Ginger didn't wait for permission and was halfway across the dance floor before Basil could comment.

She tapped on Felicia's shoulder, "Would you mind if I cut in?"

"Ginger!" Felicia said under her breath. "It's not done."

In usual circumstances, the man cut in on the dance, but Ginger prided herself on being modern and progressive. Felicia usually did, as well.

"Darling, you sound like Ambrosia." Ginger counted on the likelihood that Felicia wouldn't make a scene.

Lord Davenport-Witt smoothed over the situation. "We'll have another later on, Miss Gold, if you'll agree."

"Thank you, Lord Davenport-Witt," Felicia said, putting on a smile. "I'd like that."

Ginger willed Felicia to leave the floor before the band ended the song. The earl extended a hand, and Ginger took it.

Ginger had to concede that the earl knew his way across the dance floor. Not as skilled at the foxtrot as

Basil, but certainly good enough that Ginger could relax into the steps.

"I gather you had something on your mind, Mrs. Reed?" he said.

"I suppose it's too much to hope you'd leave Felicia alone."

"Why would you ask me to do that? Surely, you don't suspect me of anything inappropriate?"

"At the moment, everyone connected to Austin Bainbridge and Miss Kerslake is a suspect."

"But Miss Kerslake—that was an unfortunate misstep in the dark, surely."

"I'm afraid not. The police have reason to believe she was pushed. In fact, the police believe Austin Bainbridge was pushed as well, which connects the deaths. That makes you and the others who were present the days that Miss Kerslake died and Mr. Bainbridge disappeared, suspects."

Lord Davenport-Witt's face clouded. "I see."

Had he not put two and two together? Ginger wondered. Or was he playing at being naive?

"Is there anything else?" he asked as the music died down.

Ginger thought that that would be quite enough, but she had one other, unrelated question to ask. "I know I've brought this up before, but I really do feel as if we've met before."

Something flashed behind the man's eyes—Ginger was sure of it—then quickly disappeared.

"As I've said before, I'm sure I would've remembered such an encounter."

"I do not doubt your memory, Lord Davenport-Witt, only your desire to reveal it to me."

The earl's eye twitched. "If indeed we have met in the past, it mustn't be important. Otherwise, I'm certain you would recall it as well."

The music stopped, and the earl offered a polite bow. "If you'll excuse me, madam."

Ginger returned to her table as Lord Davenport-Witt left the lounge.

Felicia glared at Ginger, her grey eyes icy.

DAPHNE LOVE ENDED her song and announced the band would be taking a break so dinner could be served.

Soon the cigarette and whisky-tinted air smelled of roast duck and orange sauce.

Ginger noted how Felicia's neck constantly twisted so she could view the door, no doubt hoping Lord Davenport-Witt would return.

Finally, after barely touching her food, she leaned into Ginger. "What did you say to him?"

Ginger took her time to sip her soup. "I didn't say anything."

"He's promised me another dance but hasn't returned since you cut in."

"Perhaps something came up."

"Ginger! You warned him off me."

Ginger patted the corners of her mouth with her napkin. "Felicia darling, your timing is so questionable. We're in the middle of a murder investigation. It's not the time to flirt with suspects and plan romantic dalliances."

"I'm hardly planning a romantic dalliance."

"All I'm asking is that you wait until Basil's had a chance to arrest the killer. Then I promise to support your interests, no matter what or *who* they are."

Basil, as usual, remained quiet, but Ginger could see a look of relief in his eyes when Felicia's shoulders slumped in acquiescence.

Around the room, people ate, drank, and chatted amiably with their companions. Most did, at any rate. Adeline Bainbridge had sat alone at her table during the dancing and watched the couples with a sombre expression. One in her physical state wouldn't dare take to the dance floor, but that didn't mean she didn't wish she could. Quentin Bainbridge joined her, their son, and Lionel Findley just as the meal was served.

The chair belonging to Lord Davenport-Witt remained empty, and Ginger wondered if he were gone for good.

Ginger collected her clutch bag, the weight reminding her of the silver Remington derringer tucked away inside. The palm-sized pistol had been a gift to Ginger from her late husband when they still resided in Boston. She hoped nothing would go amiss during the evening affair, but with a murderer on the loose, it behoved one to be prepared.

"I've got to make another trip to the ladies," Ginger said.

Felicia chortled. "Again? You're going to carve a path in the carpet."

"It's one of the hazards of my condition," she said, then, turning to Basil added, "I won't be long."

Nature seemed to call every twenty minutes and was a true inconvenience. Ginger could find her way to the ladies' room in the dark, which fortunately, she didn't have to do. The weather had improved immensely, and the danger of the lights going out again due to a storm had lifted. She reapplied her lipstick and reinforced the curls of her red hair that rested under her cheekbones.

As she left the powder room, she spotted Mrs. Merrick and Mr. Floyd in conversation. The sight in itself wasn't odd as the manager and the head house-keeper often conferred, but *how* they were speaking was. Their words were too low for Ginger to hear them, but clearly, the pair in conversation was upset about something. Mrs. Merrick stormed out of the hotel with sour-faced determination.

Ginger made a sudden turn away from the lounge and towards the staircase. She avoided the lift because she didn't want Mr. Weaver to see her ascend. As quickly as she could, Ginger climbed to the top floor where the luggage was stored, and where the staff quarters were.

23

The top floor had a smaller living area than the lower two, as the roof above narrowed into the attic space where the maids and valets slept. Only four doors were present, with the second one tagged STORAGE. Ginger presumed the empty suitcases and trunks were kept there, and the one at the back of the corridor dubbed STAIRS was meant for the staff. That left two for personal occupancy, and since only the cousins lived in the hotel, Ginger wagered a guess that the female counterpart to the manager would possess the more private room furthest down the hall.

Uncertain where Mrs. Merrick had gone or how long it would be before she came back, Ginger made hasty strides to the appropriate door. Accessing her clutch bag, she removed a set of lock picks, part of her normal arsenal as a professional investigator.

Picking locks, among other things, was a skill Ginger had acquired during her stint as a secret service agent during the Great War. There were many things Ginger felt sorrow over when it came to those years, but becoming a strong, independent lady wasn't one of them.

The lock clicked open, and Ginger sneaked inside the dark living area. Using her small-sized torch, also part of her arsenal, Ginger scanned the space. She was reassured she'd guessed the correct door when she spotted female shoes by the door and feminine décor.

Though lacking the splendour of the guest suites, Mrs. Merrick's living quarters were clean and tidy. The bed was neatly made, and a well-used candle sat on a brass holder on the bedside table. Nearer to the door, a modest eating area with a small wooden table, two chairs, and a counter with a gas ring sat with a pile of crockery stacked on the side.

Ginger wasn't sure what she was looking for only that her instinct told her that Mrs. Merrick knew more than she was letting on.

The beam of her torch landed on a row of framed photographs sitting on a sideboard, and Ginger spotlighted each one. Mrs. Merrick, often grouped with a man and child, was easily recognised at different stages in her life. Ginger assumed the man and child were Mr. Merrick and their son. The most recent photographs were of an older Mrs. Merrick and a grown son, the husband no longer present.

Adjacent to the sideboard, a writing desk sat. Ginger opened the top drawer and found a stack of envelopes. Laying her clutch bag on the top of the desk, she picked up the bundle and flipped through the return addresses on the back of the envelopes. All were from a Mr. John Merrick. The housekeeper's son?

Alarm bells rang in Ginger's head. Miss Kerslake was seen with another man in 1924, and John Merrick had been registered around the same time. Had he been Miss Kerslake's beau? If so, Mrs. Merrick and Miss Kerslake had both misrepresented their acquaintance.

Ginger withdrew the stack of letters, this time reading the postmarks. John Merrick had been a consistent letter writer. One missive posted every month. The final letter was posted a year earlier, from South Africa. *Why had he gone there?* Ginger wondered, *but more importantly, why had he stopped writing?*

With a faithful son, such as John seemed to be, this could only mean that something drastic had happened to him. Under the letters was part of a damaged photograph that looked like it had been purposely torn apart —a smiling John Merrick on one side, his arm around a lady's shoulder. On closer inspection, a lady's fingers could be seen on John Merrick's waist, and the opal ring Ginger had seen Poppy Kerslake wearing was quite noticeable. According to this photograph, John Merrick and Poppy Kerslake had been more than casual acquaintances.

Clasping the envelope containing the last letter Mrs. Merrick had received from her son, Ginger debated the ethics of reading it. She loathed the thought of prying into another person's personal life, especially where deep emotion lay, but she often had to cross that boundary in her line of work. And was she not already guilty of trespassing and snooping without cause?

Not without cause, not anymore. Mrs. Merrick could be their killer, and the contents of the letters could provide motive. Ginger removed the pages, directed the beam of her torch at the neat cursive writing, and read.

DEAR MUM,

I KNOW *you didn't want me to go, but I desperately needed the distraction. I know you don't like Poppy, but I love her, and if I can make my fortune in diamonds, I know she would see me differently and love me in return. Please don't be angry with her or with me. She's just trying to make a life for herself in this world, and as you must know, a lady has fewer choices than a man has to make good. I can give her what she needs and desires. You've taught me to work hard in this life for what I want, and what I want is Poppy. But most of all, I want you and Poppy to be friends. It might take time, but it will be worth it in the end.*

I start work in the mine tomorrow. I'll write again soon.

Your loving son,
   John

GINGER'S THOUGHTS flashed to her Scout. *She'd feel horribly desperate if she ever got a letter like this one.*

Tucked inside the envelope was a newspaper clipping with the headline: MINE DISASTER IN SOUTH AFRICA.

Ginger remembered reading about this tragedy. A diamond mine collapsed, and all the workers had suffocated to death before they could be rescued. She scanned the list of names of the victims and her heart sank when she came to John Merrick.

Mrs. Merrick had means, motive, and opportunity, at least for killing Poppy Kerslake. But what did she have against Austin Bainbridge?

Ginger jumped when the door crashed open and the lights flicked on. A furious Mrs. Merrick filled the doorway.

"How dare you?"

24

*B*asil checked his watch for the third time.

Felicia laughed. "Ginger probably met someone in the loo and is happily gossiping."

Miss Love and her brass band broke into a rendition of Bessie Smith's "Lost Your Head Blues". "Why don't we dance?" Felicia asked. "She'll be back by the time this number is over."

Basil never felt at ease whilst in the middle of a case, especially one like this, but his wife had proved over and again that she could take care of herself, and he really needn't worry. Ginger would reprimand him for any sign of overprotectiveness, but he could be pardoned for being concerned about her. Ginger knew precisely how to get out of trouble because she knew how to get into it.

Felicia stared at him with bright eyes, and there was simply no way he could deny her request.

"I'd be delighted."

"I have a dreadfully long list of failed romances," Felicia said with a pout. "But perhaps it's not me who's terrible at choosing men, but rather, since the war, the selection of eligible men has been reduced dramatically."

"I'm sure there's no need for you to settle," Basil said.

"You mean with Lord Davenport-Witt?"

"I'm not referring to anyone in particular."

"It's just . . . I'm creeping up in age, and I fear I'll be a spinster if I don't act quickly. Oh, please don't tell Grandmama I said that. She'll have me walking down the aisle with some loathsome, boring creature who only has money and a title to recommend him."

Basil chuckled. "*Only* money and a title?"

"You see how difficult it is for one in my shoes. When peerage is desirable, my options are singularly reduced. I don't want to tolerate my husband; I wish to be fond of him. I wish to *love* him, and him to love me. Ginger is so fortunate to have found you."

"I don't have a title."

"Well, your father is an Honourable, and I suppose that'll do."

"That'll do?"

"If I get *close* to a title. Oh, I don't know. It's just that Lady Davenport-Witt sounds delectable."

"Are you in love with the name or the man?"

Felicia glared up at him in abhorrence. "I'm not in love with either, at present. I'm only asking for a chance."

"Perfectly reasonable," Basil said.

"See? I knew you'd understand."

"Would you be so kind as to give me time to prove his innocence? It really wouldn't go down well with Ambrosia if you link the family name to a murderer."

"Oh, Basil! But how long will it take?"

Basil's chest tightened. He couldn't answer the question because the possibility of never knowing was all too real. Many murders went unsolved, and honestly, he felt as if he were grasping at straws. How does one prove that another shoved two innocent people down the stairs to their deaths?

Basil's attention was caught by the entrance of a man in a police uniform. Constable Clarke caught his eye and lifted a hand. To Felicia, Basil said, "I'm afraid I have to end this dance early. Please excuse me."

Felicia returned to their table as Basil went to the doorway. "Constable Clarke, have you news?"

"Just a small thing, sir. It might be nothing, but Detective Inspector Attwood wanted me to pop in to answer one of your queries."

"Which one?" Basil asked.

"You wanted to know the weather report for the day that Mr. Austin Bainbridge died?"

"Righto."

"It was a clear day with temperatures up to seventy-five degrees cooling to sixty-two in the evening."

"And the tide?"

"Calm, sir. Plenty of boats were out on the water."

"Thank you, Constable."

"I hope it was helpful."

"Indeed, I think it is. If you don't mind staying, please keep an eye on things for me, and especially on Miss Gold."

The young constable's eyes lit up at the request, and the hint of a smile tugged at his lips when his gaze found Felicia at the table. "Yes, sir," he said, then glided over to their table.

Basil sighed, knowing that the young constable was about to be added to the long list of men set aside by Miss Felicia Gold.

BASIL RECALLED the manager's lie. *I would've told him the tide was too high. It was a blustery day. Dangerous for both swimming and sailing.*

Basil felt like a raging bull as he marched through

the lobby to the front desk to confront the man. When Floyd spotted him, his dark eyes shrank in fright, but then instantly, his discomfiture was removed by his typical slippery smile.

"Good evening, Chief Inspector."

"Good evening, Mr. Floyd." Basil forced professional politeness, but his mind was rapidly reviewing the facts. Floyd was all eyes and ears and knew everything that went on in his hotel. He and Gwen Merrick were cousins. He'd been vague, if not untruthful, about the person of John Merrick, and had lied outright about the weather the day Austin Bainbridge had gone missing.

"Do you recall me asking about the weather, Mr. Floyd, particularly about the day last September when Mr. Austin Bainbridge was last seen?"

"Oh yes, if I recall." He paused and threaded his fingers together. Basil waited for the lie.

"If I recall, the weather was turning sour."

"So, not conducive to swimming?"

"It probably wasn't recommended."

"Yet, later that night, the tide was out and the sea calm?"

"I suppose."

"And not too rough for sailing?"

"Well, it's never recommended to go out after dusk."

"But if one must," Basil pushed, "say if one wanted to deposit a body without being seen?"

"Sir!"

"Mr. Floyd, you lied about the weather to purposely mislead the police. The weather was fine for swimming, and more importantly, it was conducive to sailing."

"It wasn't my intent to mislead—"

"And yet, you did. I can have you charged for that."

"No, please."

"You purposely interfered with a police investigation."

"No, it wasn't like that."

"What was it like?"

"Sir, I was put in a rather difficult spot."

Understanding dawned on Basil. "You covered up for someone."

"I had to. To protect the reputation of the hotel."

"Who did you cover up for? Mr. Weaver? Mr. Cooper? No, you'd have sacked them if that were the case. Mrs. Merrick?"

Colour drained from Floyd's face, confirming what Basil had been suspecting all along. He didn't think Floyd had done the actual pushing, but he was probably a witness. An accomplice after the fact. He pressed Floyd further.

"You're guilty of one death or two, Mr. Floyd. I hereby arrest you on the suspicion—"

"No, wait! It wasn't me!"

"Who was it, then? You'd better speak up."

Floyd's shoulders shuddered, and Basil was about to grab the man by the collar when Floyd pressed his gloved hands against his eyes. "It was Gwen," he muttered,

Floyd was on the verge of a confession. Basil nudged him along.

"Gwen Merrick, your cousin?"

"Yes. She pushed Mr. Bainbridge. She didn't see me here. I was bent down behind the desk. I stood just as she sharply pushed the gentleman from behind. She tried to brush it off as accidental, saying the man was drunk, but I know what I saw."

"Whose idea was it to dump the deceased in the sea?"

"It was mine. We managed to move the body to the storage room behind the desk before anyone could see it. It was a miracle that the hotel was nearly empty at that point. A new group of guests arrived shortly afterwards.

"Oh, it was dreadful because Miss Kerslake was actively searching for Mr. Bainbridge, but once she'd gone back to her room, I sent Cooper upstairs to get

Miss Kerslake's trunk. Told him Miss Kerslake wanted it oiled.

"Once the guests were settled for the night, and Cooper and Weaver had gone home, Gwen and I packed up the body. The catamarans were locked up, so I used a bolt clipper—we have an assortment of tools at the hotel as one never knows what one might need—and we borrowed it for an hour. Afterwards, my nerves were shattered."

Basil could hardly feel sorry for the man.

"Where is Mrs. Merrick now?"

"We had a tiff, you see, I suspected she might've given Miss Kerslake a little help falling again, and she ran out of the hotel in a huff."

"She's left?"

"No, she's returned since. Never said a word to me."

Basil checked his watch, and his concern for Ginger's prolonged absence increased sharply. "Have you seen Mrs. Reed recently?"

"About twenty minutes ago, sir. I just caught sight of her as she got to the landing. She seemed to be in a hurry."

Basil spun on his heel and sprinted up the staircase.

25

Ginger blinked as her eyes adjusted to the brightness of the light. Gwen Merrick glared like a ferocious beast ready to attack. Ginger went on the offensive.

"Mrs. Merrick, forgive me. I can explain."

"There's only one reason why you'd be snooping in my things. You believe me to be guilty of murder!"

"And why would I believe that?"

"Because you and your husband are desperate to pin the deaths on someone so you can go back to your fancy home and fancy life in London."

Slowly, Mrs. Merrick closed the door behind her, turned the key in the lock, removed it, and slipped it into her pocket.

"Did you kill them, Mrs. Merrick?"

The quiet in the room resounded as each second

ticked off without an answer. Mrs. Merrick's eyes flickered to the desk, and before Ginger could intercept her, she'd made it to the object of her desire—Ginger's clutch bag.

"Wait!" Ginger ran as well, but the housekeeper was too quick, and in a flash, Ginger was staring down the barrel of her own gun. She took a careful step back.

"Ha!" Mrs. Merrick exclaimed with the excitement of her win. "You're not the only one who snoops in other people's things. I've been in your suite a few times while you were being a busybody about the hotel, Mrs. Reed. The discovery that you liked to carry this little beauty in your handbag was quite useful. And don't think I don't know how to use it. My father was a gamekeeper with no sons to teach."

The housekeeper's restrained fury seeped out with each word, and Ginger feared the woman would not be able to hold on to the intensity of her emotions for much longer. Ginger chose another approach and motioned towards the gas ring on the small counter. "Why don't we have a cup of tea and talk it over. I'll make it. How does that sound?"

Mrs. Merrick's lips tightened, but after a moment, she nodded. "No problem that a cup of tea can't solve." The housekeeper pulled out a chair and, keeping the gun at the ready, allowed Ginger to wait on her.

"This is a reversal of roles, now, isn't it?" she laughed.

Ginger filled the kettle and set it on the stove then found two teacups with matching saucers, and a bowl of sugar, all the while keeping an eye on her captor.

"No milk to be had," Mrs. Merrick said. "No refrigerator up here, so I hope you're not expecting fancy."

"Sugar is fine," Ginger said as her mind worked in the background. *Basil will be wondering where I am. It's been a good twenty minutes or more since I excused myself to use the ladies, probably longer. If he hasn't already, Basil will scout about the lounge for me then the lobby. From there, he'll go to our suite. Not finding me there, what will he do? Boss was still in our room, so Basil won't assume I've taken him for a walk, though I'd never do such a thing without letting him know my change of plans. He'll know something is amiss.*

Will he think to search the top floor?

Ginger poured the tea and pulled out a chair.

"Move it back," Mrs. Merrick said with a wave of the gun. "I don't want you close enough to pull something funny."

Ginger slid the chair back. It wasn't as if she could wrestle the gun out of Mrs. Merrick's hand. The housekeeper, though slender, was strong and fit from years of physical work at the hotel, plus having to go up and down all those stairs several times a day.

Besides, Ginger would do nothing that might put her baby in danger. She had to get away from Mrs. Merrick without the gun going off. She had to keep her talking.

"Tell me about your son," she said.

With one hand firmly gripping Ginger's beloved pistol, Mrs. Merrick kept her narrowed gaze on Ginger. She lifted her teacup with her other hand, took a tentative sip, and after lowering it back to its saucer, answered, "John was the perfect boy, the perfect son."

"You must miss him."

"Terribly. My heart is broken and will never be whole again."

"I'm so sorry for your loss."

Mrs. Merrick sniffed. "I'm not alone in this world when it comes to dead sons, but mine survived the war only to be ruined by that floozy!"

"Miss Kerslake, I presume?"

"Yes. My John met her shortly after she moved here from Australia. She was still doing small plays in London. Oh, I wish to God she'd never set foot in our country."

She waved the little pistol about without thought as she continued, "John fell head over heels for her. Lost his senses. But when she started getting famous, she dropped him like a hot potato. My John was a hard-working man, worked for the papers, but that wasn't good enough for her. No. When she left him, he was beside himself. Lost weight. Gave up his job. Then one day, he announced he was going to South Africa to make his fortune in diamonds. 'I'll come back to England a wealthy man, and then Poppy Kerslake will have me,' he'd said. Ha!"

"But why did you push Austin Bainbridge?"

"He was the one who told my son about the mine in South Africa, convincing him to go, guaranteeing John's success. Except that they'd cut corners on the proper equipment to save money, which led to the disaster. If it weren't for Mr. Bainbridge putting profits over lives, my John would still be alive."

"I'm very sorry," Ginger said with sincerity.

"I am too. You seem like a nice lady, Mrs. Reed—nicer than most of your ilk, but you put your nose where it didn't belong, and now you're a problem."

Ginger felt the threads of fear tighten. Mrs. Merrick was emotionally damaged and prone to sudden acts of violence. Ginger could be quick but not quicker than a bullet.

"Mrs. Merrick, I must appeal to your sense of motherhood. I, too, am a mother. I have a son at home, and..." Ginger lowered her hand to her stomach, "I'm expecting another child."

Sincere remorse flashed behind Mrs. Merrick's eyes. "Oh." She suddenly stood to her feet, her brown eyes darting as her mind worked for a solution. Ginger believed that the woman didn't want to kill her.

"Give me the gun, Mrs. Merrick."

"No! Stay away. They'll hang me, you know. Hang me!"

The distraught lady wasn't wrong. "Another murder won't change that."

"They don't know what I've done. They don't have any proof. Only you know because you snooped!"

Ginger's eyes were glued to Mrs. Merrick's shaky hand. "Mrs. Merrick?"

Resolve settled in the housekeeper's eyes. And then, the gun went off.

a bark from behind the door of their suite had Basil's heart racing. Boss was an exceptionally intelligent canine and one hundred percent devoted to his mistress. As far as Basil was concerned, the dog had a sixth sense. He rarely barked when he was left behind, and Basil was certain Ginger must be in trouble.

The door was locked, which meant Ginger, or someone, had locked it. If Ginger had meant to just pop in to check on her pet—not an unlikely scenario—she wouldn't have bothered to lock the door. She'd only have done that if she meant to stay, perhaps to have a quick nap?

Still, Basil couldn't believe she'd do such a thing without letting him know. Ginger was as considerate as they came, and she'd never intentionally do anything that might give him reason to worry. Just a quick look-see was in order.

Basil removed a key from his trouser pocket and unlocked the door.

"Ginger?"

Boss stood near the entrance, staring.

"Where is she, boy?" Basil said. "Is she here?"

Boss whimpered while his normally unstoppable stub of a tail didn't move.

Basil rushed from room to room. The bed was unrumpled, the quilt tightly fitted to the mattress, so Ginger *hadn't* been back to have a quick lie down. The adjoining bathroom was unoccupied, the claw-foot bathtub empty.

His brow beaded with nervous sweat, and he ran the back of his suit sleeve against it. He had to stay calm. Ginger would show herself at any moment with a perfectly reasonable explanation. It was only this blasted case causing him to fear irrationally. Besides, Ginger had repeatedly proved her clever adaptability in even the most bizarre and dangerous situations. How often had she saved his life? She had plenty of skills most women only dreamt of, due to the mysterious work she had done in the war, but not enough fear, in Basil's opinion, to keep her out of trouble.

He circled back to the sitting area, hoping that Ginger would be lounging in one of the chairs, but it was only Floyd who hovered by the door, hands clasped in front of himself.

"Is she here, sir?"

"No."

"I'm sure it's nothing to worry about," Floyd said. "Ladies tend to wander, their attentions grabbed by every new shiny thing. I bet she's left the hotel and found a dress shop which has opened late."

Basil frowned at the man's low estimation of the gentler sex, and Floyd most certainly didn't know Basil's wife. However, Basil could concede that something had caught Ginger's attention, and perhaps she'd merely lost track of time . . . if it weren't for Boss.

The animal continued to stare at him with his dark-brown eyes, an innate sense of worry behind them. When he let out a low-belly whine, Basil grew sincerely concerned.

"Mr. Floyd, where do you think Mrs. Merrick is?"

"I wouldn't know, sir."

"She has a room in this hotel, does she not?"

"Yes, we both do. On the top floor."

The housekeeper might've seen Ginger. Perhaps she could lead me in the right direction. "Take me there."

"Of course."

Basil followed Floyd into the corridor and, before he could get the door closed, found that Boss had slipped in behind him. Basil should've called for the dog himself. If anyone could sniff out Ginger's where-abouts, it would be him.

"Come on, Boss," Basil said, then to Floyd, "Please hurry along."

They'd just reached the foot of the staff staircase at the end of the hall when the blast of a gun went off.

"Ginger!"

Basil's blood went cold. He pushed Floyd out of the way and sprinted up the stairs, Boss on his heels.

"Ginger!"

Faced with three closed doors, Basil shouted, "Which one is it, man?"

Floyd pointed. "This one, sir."

Basil twisted the knob. "Blast! It's locked!" Not bothering to wait for Floyd to produce a key, he raised a leg and kicked. The door sprang open.

Basil lost his breath at the scene before him: a body slumped on the floor, a pool of blood.

"Ginger?"

His wife turned to face him. All colour had drained from her face. "She shot herself, Basil. Right before my eyes."

Basil pulled his wife into an embrace, held her tightly, and kissed her head. "I thought it was you, love. Oh heavens, I was in such a panic."

"I'm fine. It's poor Mrs. Merrick we need to think of now."

Boss sat eagerly at their feet, and Ginger bent to pick him up. "Hey, Bossy. Thanks for looking for me."

Floyd took tentative steps inside. "Gwen?"

"I'm dreadfully sorry," Ginger said. "She took my gun. I thought she wanted to harm me, but—"

Basil felt sympathy for the deceased woman, but he couldn't have been more thankful that it wasn't his Ginger lying dead on the ground. Pulling himself together, he took charge.

"Mr. Floyd, we'll have to summon the police and the medical examiner."

Floyd stared back with eyes like a wild dog then sprinted out of the room as if his life depended on it.

"Floyd, stop!" Basil took off after the manager, wondering exactly what the man hoped to accomplish. It wasn't as if he could run forever. "Floyd!"

"Is this who you're after, old chap?"

Basil nearly ran into the earl, who had Floyd gripped by the arm.

Ginger stepped up alongside them. "Oh, Lord Davenport-Witt! What are you doing here?"

"I was in my room and couldn't help hearing the commotion. It almost sounded like a gun had gone off."

"Indeed," Basil said. "One had." Without a set of handcuffs at the ready, Basil restrained Floyd by pinning his arm up behind his back. "Would you mind summoning the police and the medical examiner," he asked the earl.

The earl nodded sharply, turned, hurried down the corridor, and disappeared down the stairs.

"Would you be up to retrieving a set of handcuffs from our suite?" Basil said as he peered at Ginger. "There's a set in my briefcase."

"Certainly, darling," Ginger said. She patted her thigh. "Come, Boss, we've work to do."

27

The sun shone brightly the next morning, the same way it had when Ginger and her family arrived in Brighton only a few days before. So much had happened in such a short time that the days felt both long and short, a paradox.

Their train back to London wasn't scheduled until later that afternoon, so Ginger and Basil had a picnic breakfast on the beach. Ginger, naturally, invited Felicia, who, unsurprisingly, invited Lord Davenport-Witt.

The surprise to Ginger was that he accepted, completely upsetting her idea that he was a deceitful cad simply playing with Felicia's feelings to pass the time. Judge and jury were still out on his character, though Ginger had to admit that perhaps she'd been unduly hard on the earl, and there was a slight chance her knack for rightly judging character had failed her.

Beneath a clear blue sky, the beach was populated with deckchairs and sun umbrellas. Both Ginger and Felicia possessed a parasol to avoid those dreaded freckles brought on by the sun, but oh how tempting it was just to let one's face bask in the rays of light.

"More tea, love?"

Ginger opened her eyes and smiled at the handsome face shaded by the brim of a brand new hat. Her husband's hazel eyes took her in with fondness as she held out her teacup and saucer. "That would be delightful, thank you."

The picnic basket prepared by the hotel kitchen sat between the two couples and was nearly empty of the continental breakfast of fresh croissants, rich butter, and apricot jam, along with hard-boiled eggs, and mature cheese. Boss sat contentedly at Ginger's feet, having had his share of hard-boiled egg.

As the waves danced rhythmically to shore, Ginger replayed the events of the last few days in her mind. How tormented poor Mrs. Merrick must have been over losing her son to go to such drastic measures to avenge his death, trying, though failing, to find peace through her efforts.

Ferociously protective of young Scout, not yet twelve, Ginger couldn't imagine that changing as he grew older. Her fingers subconsciously caressed her stomach, feeling the fist-sized hard ball that had formed there over the last four months. Even though she knew nothing about the child growing within, she already knew she'd do everything she could to protect the baby from harm. The maternal instinct could be frightfully powerful.

Mrs. Adeline Bainbridge had returned to London with her husband and would soon give birth to her baby. Would Quentin Bainbridge ever learn of the true paternal heritage of his offspring? If he suspected his wife had betrayed him with his brother, would he ignore it and raise the child as his own? The baby did have the Bainbridge bloodline. Would Adeline ever confess?

What Ginger had learned about them was that neither liked to rock the boat. Nothing that was done could be undone now. Hopefully, the couple could learn to communicate better going forward. One could pray that the child would be a salve of healing and not a reminder of bitter times.

As for the Brighton Seaside Hotel, the owners had been notified of the fate of their manager and house-keeper and had closed the hotel until further notice. Ginger was pleased to learn that Mr. Weaver had no knowledge of his boss' nefarious activities, and that Mr. Cooper had only been used as a pawn to retrieve Miss Kerslake's trunk and nothing more.

Mr. Findley, of course, had been the first to depart

once the police had given the go-ahead. Ginger hoped the man would do a better job of picking business partners in the future.

"Can I tempt you with another croissant, Charles?" Felicia said.

Felicia and the earl were using Christian names, a sign that their relationship had moved from the realm of acquaintance. Ambrosia was sure to be ecstatic when she learned of this titbit. No doubt, Felicia was mentally reciting the name Lady Felicia Davenport-Witt with delight.

"Thank you, Felicia," Lord Davenport-Witt said.

From the corner of Ginger's eye, she witnessed the unnecessary lingering of their fingers as the croissant was delivered.

Basil nudged her gently. "You're frowning, love, and on such a beautiful day."

Ginger smoothed out her expression and smiled at her husband. "You're quite right."

Lord Davenport-Witt's voice reached them, but he was quite clearly addressing Felicia.

"How would you like to drive back to London with me?"

Ginger's head snapped towards the earl, who caught her eyes with a look of apology.

"I'd invite everyone if I could," he began, "but my motorcar is only a two-seater." Returning his attention to Felicia, he continued, "I know it's rather forward of me, and last minute, but I would be sincerely delighted by your company."

"I'd love to," Felicia said.

Ginger had to admire her sister-in-law's restraint as the Felicia she knew would've burst out in a girlish squeal.

"But—" Ginger started. However, Basil's light touch convinced her to stop. Felicia wouldn't be talked out of it, and anything Ginger said to stymie the earl's offer was sure to backfire.

"You don't mind, surely," Felicia said, jumping in. "I'm sure you and Basil would love some time alone, and I most certainly am tired of being a gooseberry."

"Of course," Ginger said. "We'll meet you back at Hartigan House later today." She hoped Lord Davenport-Witt got the strong hint he was to take Felicia immediately home and no detours elsewhere—such as his estate.

Lord Davenport-Witt flicked his wrist to glance at the time. "Your train is due to leave in a couple of hours," he said. "You don't mind if Miss Gold and I depart a little sooner?"

Ginger couldn't come up with a reason to hold them back. "Enjoy your drive."

Felicia took Ginger's hand and squeezed it. She

brushed Ginger's cheek with a kiss and whispered, "We'll catch up tonight."

Ginger watched as the couple skipped up the steps to the promenade and disappeared out of sight, then packed up the picnic basket whilst Basil collected the deckchairs.

"I think they'd make a nice couple," Basil said. "He seems like the perfect gentleman."

"Around Felicia, yes," Ginger admitted, "but I can't say the same about how he treated Poppy Kerslake."

"When, exactly, did he treat Miss Kerslake unkindly? From my observation, she was the one giving unwanted advances and making presumptions on Lord Davenport-Witt's time and attentions."

Ginger exhaled. "Perhaps you're right. I don't know why I've got a bee in my bonnet about the man. He's handsome, charming, wealthy, and would give Felicia a marvellous hyphenated name that will be overly long and annoying to say."

"You're not missing your title, are you, Lady Gold?"

Ginger stared at her husband, aghast. "Of course not!"

Basil burst out laughing. "I'm only teasing you, love. It's only that you sounded a little jealous of Felicia just then."

Ginger marched across the beach towards the steps. "I'm no such thing."

The fact was, Ginger worried about her memory, her intuition. She had met Lord Davenport-Witt before, she just knew it, but blast if she could put the pieces together.

Matilda Hill, with her medical knowledge, had prepared Ginger for the changes and challenges that she'd face physically, emotionally, and mentally over the next months. Ginger placed the blame for her brain strain on those.

Later, when she and Basil were travelling first class on the train to London, Ginger appreciated the fact that they had a compartment to themselves. Felicia had been right about her prediction in that regard.

The scent of Basil's cologne comforted her. Boss rested in the space beside her, his little head propped on her lap.

The steward knocked on the glass door. "I've got the city newspapers if you'd like one."

"Yes, thank you," Basil said.

Ginger contented herself with reading over her husband's shoulder. An advert jumped out at her.

"Oh, can I see that?"

"What?"

"That advertisement for the fashion show being held this summer in Hyde Park. Coco Chanel is attending! She's a fashion icon, and I follow her work religiously. I simply can't wait to meet her."

Basil grinned. "A fashion show outdoors? What if it rains?"

"Heaven forbid!" Ginger said. "It's held every year, but this summer is the first time I've been available to attend. I'm so looking forward to it. Feathers & Flair is one of the sponsors."

"Which means *you're* one of the sponsors."

"Yes. It'll be such fun."

"If you say so. I only hope you can stay out of trouble."

Ginger pulled back to stare at Basil, feigning offence. "As if I could."

If you enjoyed reading *Murder at Brighton Beach* please help others enjoy it too.

Recommend it: Help others find the book by recommending it to friends, readers' groups, discussion boards and by **suggesting it to your local library.**

Review it: Please tell other readers why you liked this book by reviewing it on Amazon or Goodreads.

Don't miss the next Ginger Gold mystery~
MURDER IN HYDE PARK

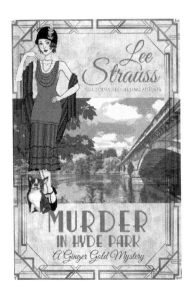

Murder's a fashion faux pas. . .

The summer of 1926 brings high fashion to Hyde
Park. Ginger's Regent Street dress shop, Feathers &
Flair, is a major sponsor, and when top designer
Coco Chanel makes an appearance, the London
fashion scene lights up.

Until a model's body is found and Miss Chanel
is suspected of murder. The fashion icon hires
Lady Gold Investigates to clear her name, but can

Ginger discover the murderer before becoming a dead mannequin herself?

Buy on AMAZON or read Free with Kindle Unlimited!

Have you discovered Rosa Reed?
Check out this new, fun 1950s cozy mystery series!

MURDER AT HIGH TIDE
a Rosa Reed Mystery #1

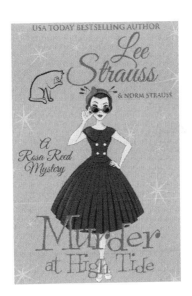

Murder's all wet!

It's 1956 and WPC (Woman Police Constable) Rosa Reed has left her groom at the altar in London. Time spent with her American cousins in Santa Bonita, California is exactly what she needs to get back on her feet, though the last thing she expected was to get entangled in another murder case!

If you love early rock & roll, poodle skirts, clever who-dun-its, a charming cat and an even more charming detective, you're going to love this new series!

Buy on AMAZON or read Free with Kindle Unlimited!

GINGER GOLD'S JOURNAL

Sign up for Lee's readers list and gain access to **Ginger Gold's private Journal.** Find out about Ginger's Life before the SS *Rosa* and how she became the woman she has. This is a fluid document that will cover her romance with her late husband Daniel, her time serving in the British secret service during World War One, and beyond. Includes a recipe for Dark Dutch Chocolate Cake!

It begins:**July 31, 1912**

How fabulous that I found this Journal today, hidden in the bottom of my wardrobe. Good old Pippins, our English butler in London, gave it to me as a parting gift when Father whisked me away on our American adventure so he could marry Sally. Pips said it was for me to record my new adventures. I'm ashamed I never even penned one word before today. I think I was just too sad.

This old leather-bound journal takes me back to that emotional time. I had shed enough tears to fill the ocean and I remember telling Father dramatically that I was certain to cause flooding to match God's. At eight years old I was well-trained in my biblical studies, though, in retro-spect, I would say that I had probably bordered on heresy with my little tantrum.

The first week of my "adventure" was spent with a tummy ache and a number of embarrassing sessions that involved a bucket and Father holding back my long hair so I wouldn't soil it with vomit.

I certainly felt that I was being punished for some reason. Hartigan House—though large and sometimes lonely—was my home and Pips was my good friend. He often helped me to pass the time with games of I Spy and Xs and Os.

"Very good, Little Miss," he'd say with a twinkle in his blue eyes when I won, which I did often. I suspect now that our good butler wasn't beyond letting me win even when unmerited.

Father had got it into his silly head that I needed a mother, but I think the truth was he wanted a wife. Sally, a woman half my father's age, turned out to be a sufficient wife in the end, but I could never claim her as a mother.

Well, Pips, I'm sure you'd be happy to

know that things turned out all right here in America.

SUBSCRIBE to read more!

.

ABOUT THE AUTHOR

Lee Strauss is a USA TODAY bestselling author of The Ginger Gold Mysteries series, The Higgins & Hawke Mystery series, The Rosa Reed Mystery series (cozy historical mysteries), A Nursery Rhyme Mystery series (mystery suspense), The Perception series (young adult dystopian), The Light & Love series (sweet romance), The Clockwise Collection (YA time travel romance), and young adult historical fiction with over a million books read. She has titles published in German, Spanish and Korean, and a growing audio library.

When Lee's not writing or reading she likes to cycle, hike, and stare at the ocean. She loves to drink caffè lattes and red wines in exotic places, and eat dark chocolate anywhere.

For more info on books by Lee Strauss and her social media links, visit leestraussbooks.com. To make sure you don't miss the next new release, be sure to sign up for her readers' list!

Did you know you can follow your favourite authors on Bookbub? If you subscribe to Bookbub — (and if you don't, why don't you? - They'll send you daily emails alerting you to sales and new releases on just the kind of books you like to read!) — follow me to make sure you don't miss the next Ginger Gold Mystery!

www.leestraussbooks.com

leestraussbooks@gmail.com

MORE FROM LEE STRAUSS

On AMAZON

GINGER GOLD MYSTERY SERIES (cozy 1920s historical)

Cozy. Charming. Filled with Bright Young Things. This Jazz Age murder mystery will entertain and delight you with its 1920s flair and pizzazz!

Murder on Fleet Street

Murder at Brighton Beach

Murder in Hyde Park

Murder at the Royal Albert Hall

LADY GOLD INVESTIGATES (Ginger Gold companion short stories)

Volume 1

Volume 2

Volume 3

Volume 4

HIGGINS & HAWKE MYSTERY SERIES (cozy 1930s historical)

The 1930s meets Rizzoli & Isles in this friendship depression era cozy mystery series.

Death at the Tavern

Death on the Tower

Death on Hanover

THE ROSA REED MYSTERIES

(1950s cozy historical)

Murder at High Tide

Murder on the Boardwalk

Murder at the Bomb Shelter

Murder on Location

Murder and Rock 'n Roll

Murder at the Races

A NURSERY RHYME MYSTERY SERIES(mystery/sci fi)

Marlow finds himself teamed up with intelligent and savvy Sage Farrell, a girl so far out of his league he feels blinded in her presence - literally - damned glasses! Together they work to find the identity of @gingerbreadman. Can they stop the killer before he strikes again?

Gingerbread Man

Life Is but a Dream

Hickory Dickory Dock

Twinkle Little Star

THE PERCEPTION TRILOGY (YA dystopian mystery)

Zoe Vanderveen is a GAP—a genetically altered person. She lives in the security of a walled city on prime water-front property along side other equally beautiful people with extended life spans. Her brother Liam is missing. Noah

Brody, a boy on the outside, is the only one who can help ～ but can she trust him?

Perception

Volition

Contrition

LIGHT & LOVE (sweet romance)

Set in the dazzling charm of Europe, follow Katja, Gabriella, Eva, Anna and Belle as they find strength, hope and love.

Sing me a Love Song

Your Love is Sweet

In Light of Us

Lying in Starlight

PLAYING WITH MATCHES (WW2 history/romance)

A sobering but hopeful journey about how one young German boy copes with the war and propaganda. Based on true events.

A Piece of Blue String (companion short story)

THE CLOCKWISE COLLECTION (YA time travel romance)

Casey Donovan has issues: hair, height and uncontrollable trips to the 19th century! And now this ~ she's accidentally taken Nate Mackenzie, the cutest boy in the school, back in time. Awkward.

Clockwise

Clockwiser

Like Clockwork

Counter Clockwise

Clockwork Crazy

Clocked (companion novella)

Standalones

Seaweed

Love, Tink

Made in the USA
Middletown, DE
17 August 2020

15831977R00139